NOT LIKE THE OTHER GIRLS

JODI ALLEN BRICE

CHAPTER 1

I smiled to myself, watching the brilliant sun quickly disappear behind the lacy limbs of the naked trees. The temperature was in the fifties but the sky was turning gray. I inhaled deeply. From my years growing up on my grandparents' farm, I knew it smelled like snow was on its way.

It was finally Christmas break and I would be heading back home as soon as I packed. As much as I enjoyed college, I was looking forward to going home for the holidays.

The heavy door of the dormitory slammed behind me as I headed down the hallway toward my room.

"Hi Kathleen!" Micah and Leslie, called out down the hall. "Are you coming to the bonfire tonight?"

I stopped at my door and smiled at the girls as I dug out my room key. "No. I'm heading home. You guys have fun." I stepped inside the room I shared with my cousin, Lori Hadler, and slung my backpack on my bed.

The tiny twinkle lights shone over my tufted headboard that my grandfather had made for me. Lori had insisted that our beds match so instead of buying a headboard, Gran and

Bumps had made it. Instead of the linen that was on Lori's, mine was made from green and cream colored toile fabric from my Gran's fabric stash.

Lori's side of the room was decorated with contemporary gold and black lamps for her desk and an expensive piece of artwork her mother, Aunt Kim, had purchased from a local artist.

My desk held a single antique green lamp my Gran had found at a yard sale and three framed pictures that I had painted when I was in high school.

It wasn't fancy, but it felt like home.

Kneeling beside my bed, I pulled out my suitcase.

The door suddenly swung open and Lori came barreling into the room. "Kathleen, you'll never guess."

I glanced up at her and grinned. Gran always told me that Lori was a tornado while I was a gentle wind. "You and Todd broke up."

She frowned. "How did you know? Did he tell you?"

I barked out a laugh and stood. "No. You guys have been fighting for weeks. And you only date a guy for about three months before you break up with him." I walked over to the calendar on the wall and tapped it. "You guys started dating in September. It's now December. It seems you are on schedule." I shrugged.

Lori sighed and laid back on her bed in a dramatic fashion. "You just don't understand. I really thought Todd was my soul mate. The excitement was there when we first kissed and he was all I thought about. But lately it's like the spark has died out." She sat up and looked at me with dramatic eyes. "Love is hard."

I shook my head. "Lori, I would hardly call *that* love."

Lori groaned. "Please don't give me that preacher's sermon about what love is. I want something more than patience and loyalty. I need excitement and longing.

Besides, if I wanted patience and loyalty, I would just get a dog."

"It's kindness, not loyalty." I muttered under my breath and opened my suitcase. We might be cousins but we were as far apart in character as could be.

My parents died in an accident when I was a toddler. They had dropped me off at my grandparents and never picked me up. I barely remembered them. My grandparents had raised me and they were the only parental figures I knew. To some it might have been weird, but to me it was normal.

"Why don't you try being single for a while. It might give you some perspective." I folded my favorite pink sweater and carefully tucked it in my suitcase.

"Single? How can I have fun if I'm single? Sorry, Kathleen. I need more out of life than reading my Bible and volunteering to drive old Mrs. Dykes to town to her doctor's appointment." She gave me a droll look. "I'm too young for that. I'm going to live my life to the fullest while I can."

I looked over my shoulder at my cousin. "I feel like I *am* living my life to the fullest."

She narrowed her eyes at me. "Just wait until you fall in love. Then you won't be so self-righteous."

"Lori," I sighed heavily. "I wish you wouldn't be so..." Offended? Sensitive? Hard-hearted?

No matter what word I used, Lori would get mad. She always did.

I couldn't help that I had practically grown up in church and it had influenced my life in such a big way.

Ever since I could remember, my grandparents had me going to church twice on Sunday and once on Wednesday. And that didn't even count the summer months when they held revivals in the small white country church with the red tin roof.

Lori and her parents went to the big church in the city when they did attend church, which wasn't very often. Her summers were spent going to cheerleader camp and an expensive vacation. My summers were spent helping my grandfather around the farm and canning vegetables with my grandmother. Lori's mom and my mom were sisters, and according to my grandmother they were as different as night and day.

Just like Lori and me.

Lori ignored me and walked over to the closet and began digging through her clothes.

My gut twisted. I hated when she was mad at me.

I stood and walked over to her. "Are you not heading home?"

"No." She lifted her chin. "I'm going to the bonfire first. I'll drive home after."

I bit my lip. "Is it going to be a big gathering?" I knew without asking there would, of course, be alcohol at the party. Lori wasn't very good at resisting peer pressure, and I didn't want her to drive home under the influence.

"It is. Matthew Hollings is going to be there." She cut her eyes at me.

I laughed. "Matthew is always at every gathering."

Lori gave me a serious look. "I wasn't going to say anything, but I overheard Lisa Durham say she's going to make a move on him tonight."

I blinked. Lisa Durham was the prettiest girl in college, and she was a known heartbreaker. It was our third year and she'd gone through ten boyfriends. She left a wake of heartbreak in her path.

I sighed heavily. "Matthew is an adult. He can make his own decisions."

Lori propped her hands on her hips and stared at me. "Kathleen. You can't be that blind."

4

I frowned. "What are you talking about?"

She rolled her eyes. "Matthew only has eyes for you."

I shook my head and chuckled. "Matthew is just a really good friend."

She huffed. "You really *are* that blind." She grabbed me by my shoulders and looked at me hard. "You're the one always talking about how you'll only marry a good man who loves God. You may say that, but I don't think you're serious. Who knows, maybe Matthew *is* that guy."

I stiffened. "What do you mean?"

Lori released her hold and pulled out a cream-colored plaid shirt and jeans. She threw them on the bed and then looked at me. "If you don't go, then Lisa is going to end up dating Matthew. Can you imagine what kind of emotional damage she'll do to him? He's totally your type. And even if you don't have feelings for him, you should go to the bonfire to at least warn him about Lisa." She grabbed her makeup and headed into the bathroom to get ready for the night.

I looked at my suitcase on my bed. I really wanted to get home, but the thought of Matthew and Lisa being together tugged at something in my chest.

I glanced at the time. I could go to the bonfire just long enough to talk to Matthew and then drive home afterward. Besides, it would be a good idea to go, to make sure Lori wasn't going to drink and drive.

Satisfied with my decision, I grabbed my phone to call Gran to let her know I would be late getting home.

CHAPTER 2

I got out of my white Chevy Impala and waved at some friends from class.

Opening the back door, I grabbed my olive green coat and slipped it on.

The bonfire was blazing with couples circling around it. I caught the comforting scent of burning embers as I walked toward the group of students.

"Hey, Kathleen!" Mike Johnson walked over and pulled me into a hug. "I'm surprised to see you here. I thought you would have headed home by now."

Mike and I were study buddies. "I had planned on it, but Lori said she was going to come to the party. And well…"

Mike gave me a knowing look. "You didn't want your cousin to be drinking and driving, right?"

"Right." I stuffed my hands in my jacket.

"Hi, Kathleen! So glad you are here! I thought you were going straight home." Micah said with Leslie at her side. They walked over and both gave me hugs.

"Yes, well. It's our last chance to see everyone before Christmas break, so I thought I'd come." I shrugged.

"Want a drink?" Leslie held out a can of beer.

"No, thanks." I shook my head. "I'm offering to be the designated driver tonight."

It wasn't a lie. I didn't drink. I never did. My parents had been killed when a drunk driver crossed the line and slammed into their car. They were killed instantly. The police saw my car seat and told my grandparents that if I had been in that car, I would have been killed as well.

"Well, look who it is. Miss Goody Two-shoes." Deacon Wilson lumbered over to our small group.

I had gone to high school with Deacon. In elementary school, he'd been a quiet kid but when he hit middle school, something had made him change. He'd become angry and lashed out at everyone. The kids soon learned to avoid him and the teachers walked on eggshells around him. He had been to the principal's office more times than I could count, and I often wondered if the reason he graduated was because the teachers just passed him to get him out of their class.

His dad had left before he was born, leaving his mother, Sarah Wilson, to raise him on her own. His mom was pretty, but always wore sadness like one would wear a shawl. She was petite and blonde and always wore long sleeved shirts even in summer. Deacon must have taken after his father with his dark hair and hard blue eyes, because he looked nothing like her.

In high school, my grandfather, affectionately known as Bumps, would always hire some high school students to help with cutting hay. Deacon had always shown up and grumbled the whole time. I once told Bumps he shouldn't hire Deacon if he was going to grumble all the time. Bumps just laughed and said words don't carry meaning, but action did. He said as long as Deacon worked, it didn't matter how much he complained.

"Hello, Deacon." Mike stiffened.

"If you think you're going to get any action out of her, you have another thing coming." Deacon smirked. "Kathleen, here, is as white as snow."

I felt my face grow beet red. In that moment, I had never hated anyone as much as I hated Deacon.

Micah and Leslie, clearly uncomfortable with the conversation, mumbled their goodbyes and quickly left.

I looked Deacon square in the face and fisted my hands at my sides. "Why do you insist on being so mean?"

"It's in my genes, I suppose." He grinned and finished off the beer he was holding.

"Hey, guys. Everything okay over here?" Out of nowhere, Matthew Hollings appeared at my side.

Deacon groaned. "Looks like the loser group is complete. I'm going to get another beer." He crumpled up his can and tossed it on the ground.

"What was that about?" Matthew frowned.

Mike shook his head. "Deacon being Deacon. I swear, one day that guy is going to get what's coming to him." He relaxed and looked at me and Matthew. "I'm going to grab some of that chili that someone brought. If I don't see you both before you leave, Merry Christmas."

"Merry Christmas." I gave him a quick hug before he sauntered away.

Matthew gave me a brilliant grin. His blonde hair and blue eyes seemed to match his endless enthusiasm. I had never seen him in a bad mood or say a cross word to anyone.

Anytime I was near him, I always felt at ease, like I was coming home.

"Kathleen, I'm glad to see you came." His eyes darted over my shoulder. "Oh, crap. Quick. Give me a hug."

He held out his arms and I laughed as he enveloped me.

"What's going on?" I hugged him back. I couldn't help but close my eyes and inhale the scent of his cologne.

Funny, I never noticed his cologne before.

"It's Lisa. She's been following me around all night."

I pulled back and looked at him. "I heard she has a thing for you. You know she's the prettiest girl on campus. All the guys are after her."

He frowned. "You're blind, Kathleen."

"What do you mean?"

He snorted. "You're the prettiest girl on campus. All the guys know it. Look around and see how many of them are looking at us right now."

I laughed and scanned the area. A group of guys were huddled in a group whispering and looking over at us. One of the guys caught my eye and grinned.

I quickly looked away.

"See. They are all wishing they were in my shoes, standing here talking to you."

I felt my cheeks heat and desperately wanted to change the subject.

"Want a drink?" He asked. "Someone actually made hot chocolate that's pretty good."

"Really? You sure it's not the instant stuff?" I arched a brow.

"Positive. Because I'm the one who made it." He smiled proudly.

"You?" Now it was my turn to be amazed.

He looked a little hurt. "Yeah, me. You think I don't know how to make homemade hot chocolate?"

"It's just unusual that a guy would know something like that."

He shrugged. "My grandmother taught me. I used to spend summers at her house. She didn't approve of me watching so much TV so she had me in the kitchen, showing me how to cook."

We walked side by side over to the tailgate of his truck.

Just as he promised there was a thermos of hot chocolate and Styrofoam cups.

I let out a laugh. "Your grandmother taught you to cook? It kind of sounds like my upbringing. My grandparents raised me."

He nodded as he poured me a cup. "I know. Lori told me when I asked where you lived."

I blinked. "You asked where I lived?"

This time it was his turn for his face to turn red. "I wanted to know more about you." He handed me a cup of hot chocolate.

"Oh." It was all I could manage to say. Had Matthew really been interested in me all this time and I never knew? I took a sip from my cup. "This is really good."

"Thanks." He graced me with a smile. "So what are your plans over Christmas break?" He sipped from his cup.

"Nothing exciting. I'll spend it at home with my grandparents. Lori and her parents will come on Christmas day, so I'll be helping Gran with the cooking. Our church makes fruit baskets for the older people in the community. I'll help pass them out with Bumps. And then there's always a candlelight service at our church on Christmas Eve that we go to."

"That sounds lovely. Like a Norman Rockwell Christmas."

I grinned. "It kind of is. What do you have planned? Going somewhere exciting? Skiing maybe?"

He laughed. "I did that last year. I told them I wasn't going with them this year."

I frowned. "So you'll be spending Christmas alone?"

"It's no big deal. I've got plenty of things to keep me busy."

I shifted my weight. "You're welcome to spend Christmas day at our house."

He brightened. "Don't tempt me. Do you really mean it?"

"Yes, but I have to warn you. It's nothing exciting. Just a

lot of home cooking and listening to stories from Bumps about when he was a kid." I grinned.

"I think that sounds wonderful." His gaze bore into mine and I wasn't exactly sure what I was feeling. It was somewhere between excitement and fear.

I took another sip of the hot cocoa. "Lori will be there so you'll know someone other than me."

"You sure your grandparents won't mind? I don't want to intrude."

I smiled. "Of course not. They'd be happy to have you."

He glanced at the ground and then met my gaze. "What about you, Kathleen? Will you be happy to have me?"

Butterflies erupted in my stomach. It was such a foreign experience I wasn't sure what to think.

All my life I'd tried to put Jesus first. It was something that had been taught to me since I was a little child. Contrary to what others thought, my beliefs had not been forced on me by my grandparents. Instead they lived their Christian life by example.

I was far from perfect and I knew that. While other girls dreamed of being successful, or marrying rich, I had always wanted a simple life with a family that pleased God.

From what I saw of the world, it wasn't something I was likely to get.

Instead I had focused on getting a degree in nursing, where I could help people the most.

Right now, as Matthew waited for my answer, I began to wonder if God placed him in my life for a reason.

I smiled. "I would love to have you over for Christmas."

He smiled and ducked his head. "Perfect. I can't wait."

Suddenly, neither could I.

CHAPTER 3

"Stop grinning at me like that." I scowled at Lori as I put the finishing touches on the dining room table. Most of the food was already on the table and the aromas were mouthwatering. I didn't eat breakfast that day, due to being so busy helping Gran, so I was ready to eat.

Gran always put out her fine china and silverware for the three main holidays, which were Easter, Thanksgiving, and Christmas. This year I had even gone so far as making placards for every seat.

"Be sure to seat Matthew away from my father. Otherwise, he might have him running for the hills." Lori's grin widened. "Although I fully suspect you'll seat him next to you, so you can have him all to yourself."

"Stop it." I hissed. "He might hear you." I glanced into the living room where Bumps, Matthew, and Uncle John were watching TV and cracking walnuts from Gran's wooden bowl.

"Somebody's in love." Lori taunted in a singsong voice.

I straightened and the heat in my face blazed as I glared at her. "I am not."

She cocked her head and folded her arms over her chest. "Then why did you invite him to Christmas dinner?"

"Because nobody should spend Christmas alone." I scowled at her.

Gran walked in and placed a sweet potato casserole on a hot pad on the dining room table. She managed to squeeze it in between the green bean casserole and the winter salad. "Kathleen is right. Everyone should have a place to go on Christmas." She smiled and looked at me. "The table looks lovely, Kathleen. I'm glad you put my mother's lace tablecloth over the linen one. It certainly brings back memories."

I nodded. "I used the antique napkin rings that Bumps gave you too."

She gave me a side hug. "Thanks, honey. Now, go tell the men it's time to eat. And tell them not to dally or it will get cold."

I grinned and headed into the living room.

Matthew looked up and smiled. "Smells good."

"Good news. It's time to eat." I cut my eyes at Bumps. "And Gran said not to dally."

Bumps let out a large laugh and stood. "Come on, gentleman. Gran has spoken." He led the way as Uncle John and Matthew followed behind him.

Aunt Kim came downstairs from the guest bedroom where she'd been wrapping last-minute gifts. "The table looks beautiful, Kathleen," Aunt Kim nodded with approval. "And you even have placards. Nice touch."

Lori rolled her eyes and plopped down at the table. She snagged a roll and took a quick bite. Her mother sent her a warning glare and she placed the roll on the edge of her plate.

"Wow, this looks wonderful, Mr. and Mrs. Johnson." Matthew smiled brightly. "Thank you again for letting me share Christmas Day with you and your family."

"We are thankful to have you, Matthew." Gran patted him on the chest. "I think your seat is over there by Kathleen."

Lori snorted. "Of course, it is."

I shot my cousin a glare but she was too busy arranging the linen napkin in her lap to notice.

As everyone found their seats, I sat beside Matthew and reached for my napkin.

"If you will bow your heads." Bumps bowed his gray head and we all followed suit.

"Dear Lord…" Before he could get any further, there was a loud knock on the door.

"I'll get it." Gran got out of her seat and went to the door.

"It's probably one of the neighbors dropping off some cookies. I can't tell you how many cookies I've eaten this week," Bumps patted his stomach. "I'm going to have to go on a diet after the New Year to get this extra weight off."

"What weight?" Uncle John laughed. "You haven't gained an ounce since I married Kim. What's your secret to staying so slim?"

"Working on a farm. There's always something to do and something to fix. It keeps me moving and active." Bumps grinned.

Gran appeared in the dining room with a tall figure in a hoodie. "Kathleen set another plate. We have another guest." She smiled wide as the figure lifted his head and I realized it was Deacon Wilson.

My stomach dropped and I blinked.

"Hello, Deacon. Glad you could make it." Bumps stood up and held out his hand. Deacon glared at me and finally shook Bump's hand before looking away.

I stood and lifted my chin. "I didn't realize we had someone else coming."

Lori groaned and crossed her arms over her chest, clearly unhappy at the sight of our unexpected guest.

"Your grandfather invited me last week." Deacon's stare went right through me, leaving me with a chill.

Bumps always seemed to try to see the good in others. This time he was just wrong. There was no good in Deacon Wilson.

"Hey, Deacon." Matthew smiled and gave Deacon a friendly wave. Deacon ignored him and looked at Bumps.

"You can sit on the other side of Kathleen." Gran patted him on the back.

I went to the china cabinet, took out another plate and went into the kitchen to gather some silverware. When I returned, Deacon was already seated beside me.

I set the plate and silverware in front of him, not caring that it wasn't arranged properly.

As I eased myself into my seat between Matthew and Deacon, I couldn't help but notice how wildly different these two guys were.

"Okay, let's try this again," Bumps grinned. "If you'll all hold hands, I'll pray."

Matthew gently took my hand and I felt my heart race. I didn't want to hold Deacon's hand but I could feel Gran's eyes on me, and I knew she would be disappointed in me if I didn't show him any kindness.

Sighing heavily, I reached over to Deacon's hand. He flinched so I pulled my hand back. Suddenly he grabbed my hand just as Bumps began praying.

Unlike Matthew's hand, Deacon's palm was rough and calloused. His grip was tight, almost painfully tight. I wanted to pull my hand away.

I didn't want to cause a scene so I didn't.

Instead, I prayed that Bump's prayer would be over so I wouldn't have to touch Deacon anymore.

As soon as Bumps said "Amen", I snatched my hand away.

"Pass those potatoes to Deacon, Kathleen." Gran ordered as she passed the green bean casserole around the table.

I held out the dish of potatoes to Deacon for him to take. He looked at me with his hard gaze and whispered in a low voice that only I could hear. "Just because your grandparents think you're being nice, doesn't mean I don't see who you are. I see you, Kathleen. Under all that righteousness is a girl wanting everything the world has to offer. No matter how wicked it is."

CHAPTER 4

I felt like I'd been gut punched. His vile words cut me to my heart and made me want to get away from him.

He was the devil incarnate. I knew it.

And Gran had let him in the front door.

"So Deacon, how is college going?" Gran looked over at him. "Do you have any classes with Kathleen?"

"I don't." He loaded his plate and began eating, effectively cutting off any more conversation.

That was fine by me. I didn't want to have to pretend to be nice to such a hateful person.

"I can't believe that we'll have to go back to school in another week. I don't think we had enough time off," Lori moaned as she cut into the slice of ham on her plate.

"You're getting more time off than they used to allow." Uncle John shook his head. "When I was your age we only had the week of Christmas off and then right back to school the next week."

"Yeah, but that was during the dark ages," Lori joked.

"Ha ha." Aunt Kim rolled her eyes at her daughter. She

looked over at me. "Kathleen, are you still planning on going to nursing school?"

I smiled and wiped my mouth with my napkin. "Yes. I'm ready for my prerequisite classes to be over so I can actually start the program."

"Nursing is a good field to go into. You'll always have a job." Uncle John nodded. "I wish I could talk Lori into going into the medical field."

"Dad, not this again." She cut her eyes at him. "I've told you there is a lot of money in getting a business degree. With a business degree I can do anything I want." She speared a piece of ham. "I might even be CEO one day."

"Honey, you have to have a company to be CEO." Uncle John smiled.

She narrowed her eyes at him. "Maybe I'll *have* my own company."

Aunt Kim fidgeted in her seat. "What about you, Matthew? What is your major?"

"My father wants me to get a law degree so I can follow in his footsteps. But I don't know. I want to do something impactful that will help people."

Gran nodded. "Fighting for people's rights is impactful. We need more good lawyers. Honest lawyers."

Bumps nodded and pointed his fork in Matthew's direction. "I think Matthew is saying he feels called to do something else."

"That's true, sir." Matthew nodded.

"You're still young. You've still got time to figure it out." Gran smiled and stood to refill glasses with sweet tea.

"What about you, Deacon?" Lori set her fork down and glared at him.

My stomach dropped and I tried to catch her eye and tell her to knock it off.

With his attitude, who knew what would be coming out of his mouth.

He sat back in his chair and grinned. "Haven't figured it out yet. Like Mr. Johnson said, I'm still young. I still have time to figure it out."

"You probably won't make it out of college," Lori mumbled under her breath. I noticed that Deacon and I were the only ones who heard her.

The smirk slid off Deacon's face and his expression hardened. "Maybe I'll own a company."

Uncle John laughed. "Yeah, and you can work for him, Lori."

Lori didn't think it was too funny, but was smart enough not to make things worse. She focused on her plate of food.

"I'm a little sad that classes start so soon. I will miss having Kathleen in the house. With just me and Bumps it gets kind of lonely." Gran pulled a face.

"Don't worry, Gran. Spring break will be here before you know it and I'll be back in time to help plant the garden." I smiled at her.

Matthew cocked his head. "So you won't be going on a trip during spring break? I know some of your friends are going to Florida."

"I went last year with them and I have no desire to go back." Since I was the only sober one on the trip, I spent the majority of the time making sure everyone made it back to the hotel room safe and sound.

Bumps smiled and lifted his chin. "Our Kathleen is an old soul, Matthew. She's not into partying like kids these days."

Lori snorted. "I'm assuming you are referring to me."

Bumps frowned. "I didn't say that, sweetheart. You know me and your grandmother are very proud of you and the young woman you're becoming."

Lori smiled at the compliment and I was relieved. Ever

since we were kids, she always seemed to thrive on some unseen competition between us. I think she was a little jealous that our grandparents were raising me, and to them I was not just a grandchild, but a daughter.

Uncle John started chatting about football which all the men, except Deacon, chimed in to give their opinion. Gran's face lit up as she talked of plans for her spring garden and Aunt Kim offered advice for the flower beds around the front porch.

When everyone had finished dinner, I stood up to grab the Hummingbird cake I'd made.

Lori followed me into the kitchen and grabbed some dessert plates. "I can't believe they invited Deacon. Did you know about this?" She whispered.

"Of course not. If I had, then I would have tried to talk Bumps and Gran out of it." I pressed my lips into a thin line. "I don't get why Bumps always has Deacon around. He's not a good farmhand and he's always complaining when he's here."

"He's never invited him to Christmas dinner." Lori shook her head as I cut the cake.

"I know. I'll talk to Gran after everyone leaves and find out what they were thinking." I placed the last slice on the plates and managed to pick up three. Lori picked up three as well and followed me into the dining room.

"Hope everyone left room for dessert." I placed a piece of cake in front of Gran, Bumps, and Uncle John. Lori gave Matthew, her mom, and Deacon some cake while I went back to grab two more slices.

I placed Lori's slice in front of her and sat down with mine.

Matthew took a bite and sighed. "Wow, this is good."

Gran smiled proudly. "Kathleen made it. It's an old family recipe that she tweaked to perfection."

Everyone, except for Deacon, went around the table complimenting my cake. He stayed silent but he ate the whole piece.

As soon as dessert was finished, Deacon stood and walked into the living room.

"How rude," Lori muttered.

I nodded, agreeing with her.

Gran shot us both a disapproving look and Bumps stood up.

He walked into the living room, and after a few seconds I heard the front door shut.

When Bumps came back into the dining room, he had a strained look on his face.

"Everything okay?" I asked.

I really wanted to know what Deacon and Bumps had said.

Had there been some words of warning from Bumps to Deacon? Had Deacon said something cringe worthy to Bumps?

I didn't want to bring it up in front of Matthew, so in the end, I kept my mouth shut as Gran ushered everyone into the living room to watch *It's A Wonderful Life*.

CHAPTER 5

I sipped on a steaming cup of hot tea as I snuggled under blankets on the bed. I watched Gran bind a quilt she'd been working on for a few months. Gran had always had her sewing machine in her bedroom instead of making room for it in the spare bedroom. She claimed she needed to keep the spare room open for visitors, which we rarely had.

The pattern of the quilt was called The Tree of Life and the colors had been done in muted shades of green and yellows. It was stunning.

"I can't believe you have to go back to college so soon." Gran sighed as she made another stitch. Her hands trembled slightly as she sewed. I'd not noticed the tremor before.

Gran and Bumps were both in their seventies, and growing up I'd always been so afraid of one of them dying before I could graduate high school. That same fear carried over to college.

I took another sip. "Spring break is ten weeks away. It will fly by."

She looked at me over the rim of her glasses. "Are you

sure you want to come home for spring break? I figured you'd want to go with your friends on vacation."

I shrugged. I've never really thought about going on vacation with my friends. But since Christmas, and hearing how Matthew was going on vacation, I had a slight twinge to go.

"Gran, I have something to ask you." I looked at her.

"Okay. Fire away." She stopped her sewing and gave me her full attention.

"I was wondering why you didn't mention to me that Deacon was coming for Christmas dinner." I tried to keep my tone casual.

"Honestly, I didn't know until your grandfather told me he'd invited him that morning." She started sewing again. "He saw Deacon that morning at the gas station picking up some Vienna sausage and crackers. Apparently his mom had worked the night shift at the truck stop and wasn't going to cook dinner. So Bumps invited him to come and eat with us."

"He certainly wasn't very grateful for the meal," I snorted.

Gran's hand stopped and she looked at me. "You can't expect gratitude from someone who's never been shown kindness."

I frowned and blinked. Her words didn't make sense. "I've tried being kind to Deacon in elementary school. I gave him half my lunch when he didn't have one. And you know what he did?"

"What?" Gran cocked her head.

"He yelled at me and threw it on the floor." I looked away.

Gran said nothing but her hand went back to making another stitch.

I didn't like the silence between us so I changed the subject. "Thanks for letting Matthew join us. I think he had a really good time."

"That's good, dear." She continued sewing.

I bit the corner of my cheek, waiting for her to ask more

questions about him. When she didn't say anything, I set my cup down and straightened my shoulders.

"Matthew does volunteer work at the food pantry as well as the homeless shelter."

"We should all help where we can." Gran nodded.

"Gran, you haven't really said anything about Matthew. He's a really nice guy and I just wanted to know what you thought of him." I clasped my hands together in my lap.

"I don't know anything about Matthew. This is the first time you've brought him home and I've never heard you talk about him before. In order for me to form an opinion of someone I need to be around them."

"So maybe I need to bring Matthew around more, is that what you are saying?" I cocked my head.

"If you like him that much, yes. People can put on a pretty face when everyone is looking. What matters is how they act when they don't have an audience." Gran stopped sewing and looked at me.

I snorted. "So Deacon must be pretty awful since he doesn't even try to hide who he really is."

Gran's expression changed to something like sadness. "Maybe he acts like that because the people closest to him have never shown him anything different. Don't be so quick to judge, Kathleen."

My mouth dropped. Her words cut me to the core. I had never thought of myself as judgmental and had tried to always be kind to everyone. Even as a child, I'd never really had a crossword from either of my grandparents.

I shoved my hurt feelings down, gathered my cup and stood. "I guess I need to go pack."

"Do you need any help?" Gran asked.

"No, I got it. You finish your quilt." I forced a smile and headed out of the room to nurse my hurt feelings.

CHAPTER 6

*T*he weeks flew by after Christmas. I was still getting good grades in my classes, and I would spend at least two nights a week hanging out with Matthew at the local burger joint.

Since Lori had found a new boyfriend a week after the holidays, she spent all her free time with him. I think his name was Jack, or it might have been John. I figured it didn't really matter because she wouldn't stay with him long.

I glanced down at my computer and then at the clock above the whiteboard in the classroom. The English professor was wrapping up his notes and I was ready for class to be over so I could pack to go home for spring break.

A piece of me wanted to go because I knew that Matthew would be hanging out on the beach with his friends with a ton of bikini-clad girls trying to get his attention. The other part of me knew I would be miserable if I went.

By the time class was dismissed, I was resolute in my decision to go home instead of going to Florida.

As I walked back to the dorm, I studied the tiny green shoots of daffodils and crocus shooting out of the ground.

Spring was my favorite time of year. It reminded me of being a child at Easter when Gran was making me a new white dress for sunrise service at church. She even bought me a white lacy hat. After church we would go home, prepare lunch then get ready for an egg hunt. Bumps always hid the eggs while I stayed inside. I think he had as much fun as I did.

"Hey, Kathleen!"

At the sound of my name, I turned to see Lori jogging toward me. I smiled and waited until she caught up.

"I guess you are headed back to the farm." Lori looked over at me as we walked.

"Going to pack up now." I cut my eyes at her. "Still going to Florida?"

"Yes." She brightened. "With Jack's parents. They have a condo in Destin."

"That should be fun." I made a mental note that her boyfriend's name was Jack.

Lori grabbed my arm. "You could come with us. I'm sure they wouldn't mind."

"Thanks, but no. I need to get back and help Gran with the garden. I think she's started without me."

Lori nodded and then her eyes went wide. "Oh, did you hear?"

"Hear what?"

"Deacon didn't come back to school after Christmas." She arched her brow.

I cocked my head. "Come to think of it, I haven't seen him around."

"Not that you would miss him. I mean he's probably the rudest guy I've ever known."

I didn't argue. Deacon was rude and mean. One might even call him a bully. I frowned. "Is everything okay? I mean why didn't he come back to school?"

Lori snorted. "Probably because he couldn't afford it anymore."

I shook my head. "I don't think that's the reason. I worked in the office at registration and in his file it stated he was getting student loans. Must be another reason why he didn't come back to school."

Lori shrugged. "Maybe he got arrested."

I started to say something but stopped. Deacon getting arrested was not out of the realm of possibilities.

We walked into the dorm and down the hallway. The excitement was palpable as students talked excitedly about their spring break plans and hurried toward the door.

I pulled out my key to open the door when Lori grabbed my arm.

"Look." She pointed to the decorative spring wreath we hung on the door. "Someone left you a note."

She grabbed the note before I could, and opened it. A slow smile grew on her face.

"Who is it from?" I scowled.

Lori smirked. "Matthew. He says he's going to miss you while he's away on spring break. He hopes you'll be thinking about him while you two are apart."

I felt my face heat. I cleared my throat. "That's nice of him." I stuck my key in the lock and turned.

Lori walked into the room and plopped on her unmade bed. "Sounds like you two are getting serious. You just might lose your V card before you get out of college." She laughed.

I jerked my head in her direction. I'd never told Lori I was still a virgin. But it wouldn't be hard for her to know since I'd never had a serious boyfriend in high school. I didn't even go to my high school prom, despite being asked. When Gran found out, she suggested I go to prom with Deacon.

I told her she was crazy. That was the first time I had remembered hurting my grandmother's feelings.

27

Lori sat on the edge of the bed waiting for me to say something. Instead I grabbed my suitcase and began packing.

"Ugh, Kathleen. Don't be mad. It's not like I'm saying something that isn't true." She rolled her eyes.

"Just because I'm spending time with Matthew doesn't mean we are dating."

She barked out a laugh. "Actually that's exactly what it means."

I spun around. "We haven't even kissed."

Her eyes widened in disbelief. "Are you kidding me?"

"No." I sighed. "Look, I'm really focusing on college right now. I've wanted to be a nurse for as long as I can remember. After that's out of the way, then I can think about having a future with someone."

Lori gave me an exasperated look. "You were born in the wrong century, you realize that right? I don't know anyone your age who hasn't had a boyfriend."

That brought a smile to my face. "Gran says I'm an old soul."

She shrugged. "Whatever. I packed last night so I'm ready to leave." She stood up and held her arms out. "Give me a hug in case I don't make it back from spring break."

I scowled at her. "Please don't say stuff like that, Lori. Not even in jest."

She pulled me into a hug and kissed my cheek. "I'm just kidding. I'll see you in a week." She grabbed her packed bag and shut the door behind her.

I glanced at the note from Matthew one last time before turning my attention back to gathering my clothes to head home for the week.

CHAPTER 7

"I wish we could grow tulips." I put the last seed in the ground and patted the soil around it. Bumps had already tilled up and prepared the vegetable garden so all Gran and I had to do was plant.

"I've never had much luck with tulips." Gran shook her head and leaned against the hoe. She'd made rows with the garden tool while I got busy planting seeds. "We are too far south here in Georgia." She gave me a smile. "But don't worry about having enough flowers growing for Easter. Our whole yard will be filled with daffodils."

Just the thought made me smile.

Every Easter our yard was abloom with daffodils as bright as the summer sun. I loved lying down in the middle of them, and staring up at the blue sky. It made me wonder how some people could not believe in our Creator. All you had to do was look around and see the intricate beauty.

"I wish they would bloom now." I stood and tugged off my dirty garden gloves. "They always make me happy."

"Is that all that makes you happy, Kathleen?" Gran eyed me closely. "You're not missing a certain someone are you?"

My face heated in embarrassment, and I turned away to pick up the numerous packets of seeds scattered on the ground. "Matthew and I are just friends."

"Friends that spend a lot of time together," she added. "Has he asked you to be his girlfriend, or whatever you young people call it these days."

I looked at her and laughed. "Are you asking if we are courting?"

She lifted her chin. "Well, yes."

"Gran, he's not asked me to be his girlfriend. We haven't even kissed."

I saw the look of relief on her face.

I knew she still saw me as her little girl, but she was going to have to let me go one day.

I heard the sound of a truck coming up the driveway. I squinted behind my sunglasses to make out who it was. It was an old white truck, with rust on the bumper, that had seen better days. I turned to Gran. "Are you expecting anyone?"

Without looking at me she answered. "Oh, that's just Deacon."

I stiffened. "Deacon Wilson? What's he want?"

"He's here to help Bumps fix his tractor."

I snorted. "What does Deacon know about tractors?"

"Kathleen! I've never heard you speak so unkindly about anyone in my life. What's gotten into you? I hope it's not the influence of Matthew Hollings."

The shock of her words had me recoiling. "You're kidding right? Do you know how bad Deacon treats people? He's always bullied everyone since we went to kindergarten. He never has a nice word to say to anyone and has only gotten worse as he's gotten older. Matthew is completely different from Deacon. He's kind and supportive. I've never heard a bad word out of him."

Gran blinked, taking in my words. "I can't judge Matthew. I've not really been around him much. I'm sorry for judging your friend, Kathleen."

Guilt washed over me. I rarely argued with Gran or Bumps, and on the few times it happened, it always made me sad. I didn't want to disappoint them.

"Why don't I go make us some lemonade?" I smiled brightly.

"That would be nice." Gran waved as Deacon got out of the truck. "And bring Deacon a glass as well."

I gritted my teeth but said nothing. Maybe silence was golden.

I jogged up the steps of our white farmhouse onto the front porch. With the winter days behind us, Gran and Bumps would soon be enjoying their first morning cup of coffee in the old white glider when the weather got warm.

I opened the screen door, letting it slam behind me as I made my way into the kitchen. The scent of freshly scrubbed linoleum floors still hung in the air from Gran's late night mopping. When she couldn't sleep, she cleaned.

I gathered up the bowl of lemons off the kitchen table and took them over to the counter. I pulled a cut glass pitcher out of the cabinet and began cutting the lemons in half.

"Your grandmother told me to come in here to get something to drink." Deacon's harsh voice was like nails on a chalkboard.

I didn't turn around but kept working. "It's not done yet."

He snorted. "How much work does it take to pour lemonade powder into a jug of water?"

I looked at him over my shoulder. "That's not how you make lemonade. You have to use fresh lemons."

I waited for him to leave but he didn't. Instead he leaned back against the kitchen wall and crossed one muddied boot over the other.

"Were you raised in a barn?"

"No, but close. I was raised in an apartment over a bar," he quipped.

I looked at him but he steeled his expression and I couldn't tell if he was serious or not.

I grabbed the lemon squeezer and began squeezing the juice out of the lemons. The juice began to compile in the cut glass pitcher. When I was done, I grabbed a pan and ran some hot water in it and put it on the stove to heat.

"What are you doing now?"

"I'm putting sugar in the water so it will dissolve."

"Why don't you just dump it in the pitcher?"

"Because it would take longer for the sugar to dissolve and it won't taste as good." I slowly stirred the sugar water until it began to boil. After making sure the sugar was dissolved, I poured the mixture in with the lemon juice and then popped a couple cubes of ice in before stirring again.

"Now it's ready." I turned to glare at him but he'd moved from his position against the wall.

He was standing right behind me. He was too close, close enough for me to smell the sweat on his chest. I tried to step back but the counter was there.

My heart beat in my chest, harder than it ever had. For the first time in my life I was afraid.

He narrowed his hard eyes on me.

"What do you want?" my voice sounded oddly calm. What I wanted to do was scream.

"I want what I was promised." He reached behind me to pull me close to him.

"Touch me and I'll scream."

He gave me an odd look and then picked up the pitcher of lemonade. He grabbed one of the coffee mugs hanging on the rack and poured himself a generous amount. He tipped the cup and drank the entire thing.

When he was done, he set the lemonade pitcher down and shoved the cup in my hands.

He shrugged. "I've had better." With that, he turned on his heel and headed out the back door.

My fear turned to hatred. I wanted to pick up the glass he drank from and throw it to the floor to break it into a thousand pieces.

But in the end, I didn't. Instead, I poured two glasses of the best homemade lemonade I'd ever made and took them to my grandparents.

CHAPTER 8

I was out for summer break, and I couldn't have been happier. I had lined up a part-time job, on Fridays and Saturdays, as a cashier at the local hardware store. While some girls would balk at the idea of such a job, I found joy in helping customers find the right paint for their living room, or seeds for their garden, or plant for their porch. Helping someone with their home always made me feel good.

Lori didn't work during the summer break. Instead she was planning on doing a couple of vacations with her friends.

I inhaled deeply. The scent of oil, paint, and fertilizer seemed to always permeate the store. In some ways it reminded me of the farm. Maybe that's why I liked working there so much.

"Kathleen, can you help Mrs. Fields with some plants out in the garden area? I have to get this new shipment of mulch unloaded." Mr. Adam Killebrew gave me a hopeful smile. He and his wife, Michelle, owned the store and were well into their sixties, and had no plans to retire.

I nodded and smiled. "Sure, Mr. Killebrew." I headed into the garden center and found Mrs. Fields squinting as she looked between two pots of petunias.

"Hello, Mrs. Fields. Can I help you with some flowers for your front porch?"

Mrs. Fields looked at me and smiled. "Hello, Kathleen. How's your grandmother? I missed her at Sunday school last week."

"She had a bit of a cold and didn't want to spread it. She's better now. Thank you for asking." I looked at the petunias. "This one will cascade over the side as it grows. And this other one won't."

Mrs. Fields looked at me and nodded. "I think I want to get two that cascade. I want to put them in those large containers on either side of my door."

I nodded and smiled. "Those will be beautiful. Have you thought about adding another plant, something with height in the back?"

She frowned, shaking her head.

"We just got some fresh ornamental grass that is really pretty. And they are on sale this week."

Mrs. Fields perked up. "Really? I think I'll have a look then."

"If you need anything else, let me know. I'm going to set your petunias up front by the register."

Mrs. Fields smiled as she toddled over to the ferns.

"Can I help you with that?" A familiar voice had me turning around.

"Matthew? What are you doing here?" I gaped.

He grinned. "I stopped by your house but your grandmother told me you were working today." His eyes ran down me and for the first time ever, I felt self-conscious about my paint splattered jeans and red T-shirt.

"Yeah. I work every Friday and Saturday."

He shoved his hands in his jeans and rocked back on his heels. "What time do you get off?"

"Five. Why?"

He gave me a bashful look that went straight to my heart. "Because I want to take you out on a date. A proper date. Dinner and a movie?"

I grimaced. "We don't have a movie theater in town."

His eyes widened at such a notion and then he nodded. "So what do you do for fun around here?"

I knew his idea and my idea of fun were as far apart as the East was from the West.

"Well, tonight I was supposed to help Gran take some food to our church. They are having a dinner to help raise money for Mr. and Mrs. Jordan. The wife has cancer, and the church is selling plates to help with the cost of traveling to and from treatment."

His eyes brightened. "What kind of food will there be?"

I chortled. "Anything from fried chicken to pot roast and that doesn't include the sides like macaroni and cheese and mashed potatoes, just to name a few."

"All homemade?" He cocked his head.

"Of course. No self-respecting Southern lady would bring anything less."

His grin deepened. "So how about dinner at the church and then a walk. I noticed there's a park on the town's square."

I gave him a skeptical look. "Are you sure that's what you want to do? I mean it's not exciting like you are used to."

He took a step closer. "As long as I'm with you I don't care what we do."

My face heated and I shoved a strand of my hair behind my ear. "Pick me up around six?"

"Great." He glanced down at his jeans and button-up shirt. "Is this okay to wear to church?"

I grinned. "It's perfect."

CHAPTER 9

$\mathcal{I}$ glanced down at my sunny yellow sundress and then back at my reflection in the mirror. I'd thought about pulling up my thick brown hair into a ponytail, but decided just to leave it down. Instead I used the curling iron to create some soft curls.

I added some mascara with some pink lipstick and headed downstairs.

"Kathleen, you certainly look lovely." Bumps smiled. "Maybe too dressed up for our little supper at church."

Gran eyed me. "Dear, I'm sure she's dressing up for Matthew."

Bumps eyebrows shot up. "Oh, yeah? I didn't know he was coming. Must have driven a long way to get here."

Gran's lips pressed into a thin line. "Seems like he's pretty serious about Kathleen."

"Gran, we're just friends." I assured her. The truth was, I wasn't sure what we were. We spent a lot of time together at college, he made me laugh, yet he never tried to kiss me.

"It's good Matthew will be there." Bumps smiled. "It will be good for Deacon to have another familiar face at church."

My stomach dropped. "Deacon will be there?"

"Of course. I invited him yesterday when I ran into him in town. That boy looks a bit on the skinny side. Told him to come on to the church and I would buy him and his mom a plate." Bumps frowned. "Although, I doubt his mom will show up. Haven't seen her around town in a while. I guess he can take hers to go."

My dreams of a perfect night went up in flames.

There was a knock on the front door. Bumps smiled. "I'll get it."

He opened the front door to Matthew standing there holding a bouquet of red roses.

"Hello, Matthew. Good to see you again. Come on in." Bumps greeted him amicably.

Matthew stepped inside and shook hands with my grandfather.

"Hello, sir. It's good to see you again." He smiled and then his gaze drifted over to me. "Wow, Kathleen. You look beautiful."

My face went red and my stomach trembled.

"Hello, Matthew." Gran stepped up and gave him a quick hug.

"Hello, Mrs. Johnson. I hope you both don't mind me joining you for this dinner at church."

Gran smiled. "Of course not. The more the merrier. Well, if you excuse me I need to get these pies loaded into the car."

Bumps grinned. "That's my cue to help." He excused himself and followed Gran into the kitchen, leaving us alone in the entryway.

Neither of us said anything. I bit my lip and then looked at the flowers. "I'm guessing those are for me."

He blinked and then laughed nervously. "Yes, they are." He held them out.

I gently took them. "Thank you. They are gorgeous."

Gran and Bumps passed us with pies in their hands. Gran turned to look at me. "Will you and Matthew follow us to the church?"

"We'll be going as soon as I get these in some water." I headed into the kitchen to find my favorite vase.

I bent and opened the cabinet under the sink. I found the tall pink cut glass vase.

"Am I dressed too casual?" Matthew asked.

I looked over my shoulder and grinned. "No. Jeans are fine. It's not a church service." I ran some water in the vase and began arranging the roses.

"You look beautiful."

He had stepped closer and I could feel his breath on my neck. A shiver went up my spine. "You already said that," I managed to say.

I cleared my throat and turned to face him. "I guess we should be going."

His eyes darkened and his gaze landed on my lips. I felt my heart quicken and I wondered if it would jump out of my chest. Not out of fear, but out of excitement.

He reached for my cheek and brushed a curl away from my face. Ever so gently he cupped my face with one hand and pulled me close with his other hand on my hip. I could feel his warm breath on my lips before he kissed me.

It was slow and gentle and I couldn't help but give way to the kiss. Everything seemed to be moving fast and slow at the same time. The sound of my heart, the feel of his lips on mine, the sensation of his hand holding me close against his body.

It was like time had stopped as we touched.

I heard the honk of a car and I pulled back. Gran and Bumps were still outside waiting on us.

"I guess we better go." Matthew's words were breathless as he caressed my cheek.

I nodded.

He finally released me and took a step back, as if he didn't trust himself to not keep kissing me.

I liked that feeling. The feeling that I was desired and wanted.

It made me realize something else, something that scared me.

I was falling in love with Matthew Hollings.

CHAPTER 10

*W*hen we pulled up to the church, it was a full parking lot. My excitement over the kiss had turned to nervousness about what Matthew might think of our church.

We were a simple country church, certainly not a big fancy church that I'm sure he was used to attending.

We got out of his car and I looked at him to try to gauge his thoughts.

"It's pretty. Looks like something out of a Norman Rockwell picture." He nodded and looked at me.

I relaxed a little. I wanted him to like it. Church was a big part of who I was. I would be heartbroken if he didn't have the same convictions about God that I had.

He gave me a bright smile. "Let's go in and get a seat."

I relaxed a little as we walked up the steps. He rested his hand at the small of my back and I couldn't stop blushing.

We stepped inside the empty sanctuary. Voices drifted in from the back of the church where the fellowship hall was located.

Matthew looked around at the stained glass windows and

smiled. "It's actually quite pretty. I could see how someone would never want to leave a place like this."

I cocked my head. "Really? You're not changing your future occupation from lawyer to preacher are you?" I grinned.

He blinked and started to say something, just as the door opened. We turned to look behind us.

"Deacon, I didn't realize you would be here." Matthew stated. He took a step toward him and held out his hand.

Deacon narrowed his eyes, closed the distance, and looked down at Matthew's outstretched hand.

Deacon didn't shake his hand. "Why are you here?"

Matthew dropped his hand and lifted his chin. "I came to see Kathleen."

Just then the door to the fellowship hall opened and Bumps appeared. "There you two are. We were starting to get worried." His gaze drifted over to Deacon. "Glad you could make it, Deacon. I've got to get the rest of the pies out of the car, can you give me a hand?"

"I'll help." Matthew offered. He leaned toward me. "I'll be right back."

Dread oozed into the pit of my stomach. I didn't want Matthew to leave me alone with Deacon. Who knew what he would do.

"Thank you, Matthew." Bumps smiled and patted my arm as he passed by.

I watched as they walked out the front door and closed it behind them.

I turned to go to the fellowship hall, but Deacon grabbed my arm, stopping me.

"Why are you dressed like that?" He narrowed his eyes on me.

"Like what?" I cringed and pulled out of his grasp.

"Like a daffodil. You're wearing makeup too. You never wear makeup." His eyes were full of accusations.

I blinked back tears at his mean words. "It's just mascara and lip gloss. Why do you even care?"

"You look ridiculous." He sneered.

I felt tears threaten to fall. I didn't want Deacon Wilson to know he could cause me such pain. If he knew that, then he would spend the rest of his life making me miserable.

"Why do you have such an interest in my life? You're not a stalker are you?" I fisted my hands at my sides and glared right back at him.

He let out a dark laugh. "You're so conceited, Kathleen. You think all the guys want you. The truth is none of them do. Especially me." He snorted and walked back into the fellowship hall.

My face burned with embarrassment and hatred for the one man in the world that I wished would fall off the face of the earth.

I didn't know why God would have put Deacon in my small town. All I knew was that I was going to avoid him for the rest of my life.

CHAPTER 11

*A*fter Matthew kissed me that day in the kitchen, we had been inseparable. On the days I worked, he would call that night and we would talk for hours. On the days I was off, he would always show up at the farm. Bumps always seemed delighted to see him, but Gran always seemed put out. I couldn't figure out why she didn't adore Matthew like everyone else who met him.

Summer had flown by and I was in my room packing my clothes for college. I was finally starting nursing school and I couldn't wait to start clinicals.

Gran walked in and sat on my bed. "Don't forget to take your journal. And your quilt. I mended the binding so it will last you a little longer." She rubbed her finger along the patchwork quilt on my bed.

"I won't forget, Gran." My stomach twisted. Our relationship had changed over the summer. We hadn't spent as much time together as I expected. I still helped with the farm and spent much of my time there, but Matthew was there as well.

He was coming over so often and his house was over two hours away. There had been a handful of nights that Gran

JODI ALLEN BRICE

had let him sleep in the guest room. Oddly enough, I was excited and scared that he was so close. While we kissed every time we had a chance, it had never gone any further.

He said he wanted to wait until the right time. And when he said those words, I knew in my heart he was talking about marriage.

I'd never experienced that kind of love with anyone before. As much as I wanted to wait until we were married, I didn't know if we would be able to wait. The way he kissed me and held me let me know he wanted me as much as I wanted him.

Surprisingly enough, he never snuck into my bedroom.

I think it was out of respect for my grandparents. Either that, or he knew if Gran or Bumps had caught him in my room, they'd kill him or at least make him wish he were dead.

I saw another change in Matthew that surprised me. He came to church with us every Sunday and sometimes on Wednesday nights. He seemed to drink in every word the preacher said and even asked him questions after the service was over.

"I noticed Matthew chatting up the pastor last Sunday. Wonder what they were talking about?" Gran glanced around my room.

I stopped folding my clothes and looked at her. "I'm not sure. He didn't tell me."

"Kathleen, is Matthew a Christian?" Gran gave me a pointed look.

Her words startled me. I laughed a little. "Yes. I mean he's been faithful to come to church with us every Sunday. And he said he was baptized when he was twelve."

She looked at me for a long time and then picked up one of my T-shirts and began folding. "I'm guessing you think you're in love with him."

46

I cocked my head. "What if I am? Would that disappoint you? Me finding someone who loves me?"

She looked up at me, pain etched around the corners of her eyes. "Love is more than an emotion. It's following through, and staying committed, and doing the hard things even when you don't feel like it."

I blinked and then eased onto the bed beside her. I took her wrinkled hand in mine. "Gran, I've never really thought about marriage until I met Matthew. I always thought about getting my nursing license so I could help people. And to be honest, I wasn't really interested in Matthew as a boyfriend. We started out as friends and it just led to something deeper."

She gave me a sad smile. "I just hate losing you."

I smiled and pulled her into a tight hug. "You'll never lose me. I'm always here for you and Bumps. Besides, it's not like he's even asked me to marry him. I think you're putting the cart before the horse." I chuckled.

Gran's face grew pensive. "He'll ask you. I have a feeling. And I also know what you'll say." She got up and headed out of my room.

I sat there wondering why it hurt so much that Gran didn't see Matthew the way I saw him.

I'd met his mother and father on two different occasions when he took me out to dinner. It was obvious he came from money, from the looks of the expensive jewelry his mom, Kitty, wore and the designer suits his father, Jack, wore. I always felt a bit uncomfortable when I was around them because of the discrepancy in our financial situations. They went out of their way to be kind and soon I had a comfortable relationship with them. His grandmother had passed a few years ago so he seemed to miss her terribly. I think maybe that's why he wanted Gran's approval so bad. When you were in her good graces, she smiled for days.

Except lately, Gran's smiles were few and far between.

CHAPTER 12

T cracked my eyes open at the first rays of light coming through my window. I smiled and looked around at my room, reminding myself I was back home. My first year in nursing school had left me exhausted. Trying to balance a relationship with Matthew and keep up with my studies had proven difficult. Despite all that, I managed to keep my stellar GPA and was now ready for a summer break. My job at the hardware store awaited me and my grandparents were thrilled to have me back home.

I swung my legs over the side of the bed and stood. I was grateful for the cool hardwood floor underneath my feet. I could already tell from looking outside that it was going to be a scorcher outside today.

"Kathleen, breakfast is ready." Bumps called from downstairs.

I hated to tell him that since going to college, I rarely ate breakfast anymore, instead surviving on coffee to get me going. I quickly threw on some shorts underneath the T-shirt I'd slept in and hurried downstairs to the kitchen.

The scent of bacon and biscuits hung heavy in the small

kitchen. Gran smiled when I appeared in the doorway and held up the coffee pot. "Ready for some coffee? We've got a big day ahead of us."

"Coffee sounds divine." I smiled.

"Sit and I'll pour you a cup. Sugar and cream are already on the table." Gran filled the brown coffee mug as I sat.

I made quick work of doctoring up my coffee before taking my first sip.

I brought the mug to my lips and tasted. A sigh slipped out.

"Missed my coffee, did you?" Gran grinned.

"You have no idea. Hospital coffee is awful." I settled in my chair and gazed out the back door.

Summer was in full swing with Gran's rose bushes trying to climb the railing on the wraparound porch.

Besides having a lush vegetable garden, Gran also took pride in her flowers all around her house.

"I need to trim the roses back." I cocked my head. "Is that a new color coming up beside the pink rose bush?"

Gran followed my gaze. "It is. It's a Jacob's Coat of Many Colors. My neighbor gave me a cutting a few years ago and it's just been growing like a weed. This is the first year it has bloomed."

The unusual rose with its merging colors of pink and orange and yellow was stunning.

Bumps loaded our plates with bacon, biscuits, and gravy. "Hope you're hungry." He set the skillet on the stove and sat down.

"Bumps, I haven't eaten a meal like this since high school."

"Well, looks like you need it. You're way too skinny." He picked up my arm and wrapped his thumb and finger around my wrist.

I rolled my eyes and slid out of his grasp. "I've been too busy to eat. Not to mention the stress of school."

Gran frowned. "Do you think you made a mistake going into nursing?"

I quickly shook my head. "Oh, no. It's not that. It's just hard trying to study and go out with Matthew and all."

Bumps took a bite of his bacon. "I hope Matthew's being supportive of your dreams, dear. You've talked about being a nurse since you were a little girl."

"Oh, he's supportive. It's just hard when he's so far away and my hours during clinicals are long. Just trying to make everyone happy." I found myself taking a bite of my biscuit so I couldn't answer any more questions.

There was a knock on the front door. I jumped up before anyone else. "I'll get it."

I hurried to the door, grateful for the interruption. I was so relieved that I threw open the door without looking to see who was there.

I came face to face with Deacon.

"What are you doing here?" The words tumbled out of my mouth before my brain could catch up.

"Good morning to you too," he said dryly.

I lifted my chin. "I'll tell Bumps you are here." No doubt my grandfather had hired him for some odd job around the farm. Bumps had the patience of Job when it came to dealing with miserable people like Deacon.

"No need. I'll tell him myself." He shoved the door open wide and walked right past me.

Irritation flared in my gut. I shut the door and grabbed his arm. "Look, I don't know what kind of arrangement you have with my grandparents, but I don't want you coming over here to take advantage of them. I don't even know why you are here."

He narrowed his eyes on my hand clutching his arm.

I let him go and folded my arms around my chest.

"Deacon! Good morning." Gran peeked her head through

the doorway. "Come on in the kitchen and get some breakfast."

"Thank you," Deacon said, but kept his gaze and his smirk on me.

Gran disappeared back into the kitchen.

"You know, you really should be more hospitable like your grandparents." He narrowed his eyes.

"I'm hospitable to people who deserve it." I lifted my chin.

A brief look of hurt passed through his eyes before he shuttered his expression. "There's the real Kathleen you try to keep hidden from the world. Everyone thinks you're so nice, but you have everyone fooled, don't you?"

I opened my mouth to say something, but nothing came out.

He gave me one last look before heading into the kitchen.

Angry with him, and with myself for not telling him off, I stormed upstairs to get dressed for the day.

CHAPTER 13

Sweat rolled down my face as I cut and wrangled Gran's rose bushes into submission. I had started in the vegetable garden, weeding and picking any fresh produce. Usually, I would go to the barn to see if Bumps needed any help working on the tractor he'd had for years, but since Deacon arrived, I steered clear.

With him at the farm, my good mood was lost and I wanted the day to end so he could go home. I wanted Gran and Bumps to myself.

Deacon Wilson was an intruder in my perfect world.

The screen door slammed and Gran stepped out on the porch. "You got a lot done, Kathleen. Here, have some lemonade." She held out a glass of the refreshing beverage.

I gave her a grateful smile. "Thanks, Gran." I took the glass and drained half the contents. I swiped my brow and sat down on the steps. "Gran, can I ask you something?"

"Sure, honey." She sat in the wicker rocker and looked down at me.

"Does Deacon come over a lot?"

Gran shrugged. "Whenever Bumps needs help, he comes over."

I snorted. "I'm guessing he's not doing it out of the kindness of his heart." Deacon Wilson didn't have an ounce of kindness in his entire body. "I would think he would have gotten a job since he dropped out of college."

'Oh, Deacon works. He just comes over to help when he can." Gran set the rocker in motion.

"Really?" I took another drink. "Where does he work?"

Gran frowned as if she were in deep thought. "He's never really said. But he works out of town during the week and is only home on the weekend."

I frowned. He was probably doing something illegal like stealing cars and selling them. In high school he had an old Camaro that he had fixed up. I noticed when he arrived today he was driving an old Ford truck which had been lifted. He probably loved his vehicles more than people.

"Has Matthew called today?" Gran looked out over her land.

"No. I'm sure he's busy. We told each other we were going to make sure to enjoy our summer with our families and not stress about going out every week." I hated to admit it but I already missed Matthew. But I knew that throwing myself into work around the farm helped keep my mind and heart occupied.

"Hmmm." Gran kept rocking. "So what's your plan for the summer? Not taking any extra classes?"

"No. I need a break. I still have my regular hours at the hardware store on Friday and Saturday, and I think I can pick up some extra days as needed. Summer is always a busy time for the store." I shrugged. "Other than that, I plan on helping out a lot around here."

Gran smiled. "I'm glad Kathleen. I'm not as young as I

used to be and I can certainly use the help. Especially when we start canning."

I grinned and rubbed my hands together. "I can't wait to get started. I already have a lot of plans for all the vegetables we will put up this year."

Gran laughed. "You are the only girl your age that thinks about canning vegetables, Kathleen. Just look at Lori. All she thinks about is finding the next boyfriend and going shopping." Gran's expression went serious. "Speaking of shopping. Are you sure you don't need another uniform for clinicals? I've worried myself to death thinking that you can get by with two sets of uniforms. Do the other girls have more?"

I snorted. "I have no idea, Gran. I've never asked the other girls. Besides, I wash my uniform when I get home so I'll always have a clean one to wear." I stood and handed the glass back to her. "You worry too much."

"Well, I'm supposed to. It's part of my job." Gran stood and headed inside.

I swiped at the sweat from my forehead, grabbed my large shears and headed back to work.

The sun was hot overhead and seemed to beam down on me. Growing up in the South I was used to the heat but this summer it seemed unusually hot.

I worked feverishly, lopping off the unwieldy rose bush tendrils until the bushes looked neat and orderly.

Once I was done, I headed inside to help Gran with her housework.

CHAPTER 14

The summer had passed too quickly and I was packing for college when I heard a car pull into the driveway. I shoved the white lace curtain aside and peered out.

I didn't recognize the Toyota but I recognized the driver when he got out.

"Matthew," I sighed.

I glanced at my reflection in the mirror. My faded jeans and white flowing blouse made my blue eyes pop. I patted down my dark brown hair and quickly put on some mascara.

By the time I was done, I heard footsteps coming up the stairs.

Gran appeared in my doorway. "Matthew is here to see you."

I nodded. "I'll be right down." I didn't want to appear too enthusiastic so I took my time putting on my shoes. Thankfully I polished my toenails last night in a pretty plum color. It complimented the tan I'd gotten over the summer from working in the garden.

I cast one last glance in the mirror before heading downstairs.

Matthew was standing at the bottom of the stairs looking up at me.

He brightened when he saw me.

My heart quickened as I hurried down the stairs. He took my hands in his and gave me a kiss on the cheek.

"Hi. I wasn't expecting you to drop by. I was just packing before I head back to college."

He nodded. "I was trying to get here before you left. I need to talk to you."

I frowned. "Okay. Let's go out on the porch." I led the way to the front door and stepped outside.

Matthew followed.

We sat down in the white wicker swing at the end of the porch near the window of the living room. I squinted to see if Gran or Bumps were close enough to hear us but I didn't see either of them.

"What's going on? I figured you would be back at your dorm already."

He took my hand in his. "That's what I want to talk to you about."

"Matthew what's going on?" I angled my body toward him, giving Matthew my full attention.

"I'm not going back to law school." He swallowed hard.

"You're not? But it's your dream." I couldn't comprehend what he was saying.

"It's my parents' dream. Not mine. Never was. Look, Kathleen, since I met you I realize there is so much more to life than making money and buying a big house. I've never really been around someone who doesn't focus on the importance of money, or status in life, or material things. And all this time that I've spent with you this summer, it made me realize something. I want to do something good with my life, something that matters." His face broke out into a wide grin. "I'm going to seminary school."

I blinked. "You're what?"

He nodded enthusiastically. "After talking to Pastor Thomas at your church, I realized how much I can do to help people. By becoming a pastor."

I blinked.

His smile faded. "Kathleen, I thought you'd be thrilled. You'd be helping people through nursing and I would be helping through preaching the Word of God."

I shook my head and laughed a little. "I'm sorry, Matthew. It's not that I'm not happy. I am. Becoming a pastor is a true calling. The life of a pastor isn't always easy but it's always rewarding. If this is what you truly feel called to do, then I'm thrilled, Matthew." I hugged him tight.

"That's what I was hoping you would say." He whispered against my ear. When he pulled away he took my hands in his. "Now I have something else to say."

I laughed. "What else could possibly top what you just told me?"

He grew serious and stood up. He pulled a small box out of his jean's pocket and knelt at my feet.

I felt all the blood drain from my face. Everything seemed to be going in slow motion.

He opened the small blue box exposing a large diamond engagement ring. "Kathleen, will you marry me?"

My mouth dropped and I gasped. Tears burned behind my eyes. Tears of joy, tears of surprise, tears of uncertainty.

"Oh, Matthew." I buried my face in my hands and began to weep, overwhelmed with emotion.

"Sweetheart, are you okay?" He took my hand in his.

I looked at him through my misty eyes, and nodded fervently.

He breathed a sigh of relief. "Good. That's good." He

cleared his throat. "Kathleen, I kind of need an answer." He gave me a worried look as if I were going to reject him.

I threw my arms around his neck. "Yes, of course, I'll marry you."

In that moment, I wasn't sure about much. I wasn't sure if we would have a long engagement so we could both finish school. I wasn't sure if we'd get married right away and find some way to make college work for both of us. I wasn't even sure where we would live since neither of us had any money.

All I knew was that God had put Matthew in my path and he was the man I was supposed to spend my life with. How could I say no to that?

$\mathcal{A}$fter we broke the news to Bumps and Gran, I could tell they were totally taken by surprise. Bumps hugged us both and congratulated us. Gran forced a smile and headed into the kitchen to pour us all some lemonade.

I knew she was hurt that Matthew didn't ask for my hand before proposing. It was hard to explain to her that these were modern times and that tradition was outdated. I didn't say anything because I didn't want to hurt her feelings any more than I already had.

We had agreed to hold off on wedding plans since we were both still in college and needed to focus on that first. We agreed that we would marry after we graduated which pleased my grandparents greatly.

I found myself submersed in my clinicals and tests at nursing school. Matthew tried to call every night but his calls soon dropped to every other night and texts on the nights we didn't talk on the phone.

When we did talk on the phone, we chatted about our future, where we would live and how many children we would have.

I wanted to live near my grandparents and have four kids while Matthew preferred two children and living in a big city.

In the end we both agreed it didn't matter where we lived or how many children we had, as long as we had each other.

Matthew's parents had seemed thrilled about the engagement, but not so sure about Matthew's change in career plans. His mother even tried to get me to convince Matthew to go back to law school. Of course I didn't. It was his decision and who was I to get in the way of it.

As happy as I was about the engagement, I was stressed about nursing school. I had to arrive at the hospital early for clinicals and study during any free time I could find. The next couple of years flew by faster than I anticipated. Before I knew it I was walking across the stage and getting my RN degree.

Matthew, my grandparents and Matthew's parents, along with my Aunt Kim and Uncle John, and of course, Lori, were all there to see me graduate. It was one of the happiest days of my life.

I had been applying and interviewing for jobs and so far I had been offered a position in three different hospitals.

It was hard for me to choose because I had not discussed it with Matthew.

He said seminary was harder than he anticipated. His visits grew more sporadic as time went by. He said studying had to take precedence if he wanted to be successful and pass with flying colors. I completely understood, and even offered to drive the four hours to visit on the weekends, but he told me not to. He would be studying and we really wouldn't have time to spend together.

As much as I missed him, I was totally supportive.

Everything we were doing was for our future. Him a minister and me a nurse.

What better careers could we honor God and help those who were hurting the most?

CHAPTER 16

I put the finishing touches on the dinner I had cooked for Matthew. Gran and Bumps were over at the church helping with organizing a fundraiser for a neighbor that needed some financial help due to medical bills. I was going to go, but Gran insisted on me staying home so I could spend some quality time with my fiancé.

It was Saturday night and Matthew was on his way over from seminary. I knew he had been studying hard the last few weeks for a test he'd taken yesterday. He said he needed some downtime and couldn't wait to see me and spend some time together.

I heard the car pull into the driveway. Letting out a squeal, I tossed my apron on the dining room chair and ran to the front door to greet him.

He grinned as I threw my arms around his neck and squeezed him tight.

"I missed you," he whispered against my ear.

"I missed you too," I pulled back from our hug and our lips met.

The kiss was intense and needy. It scared me how much I could love and want someone so badly.

We pulled away and breathlessly looked at each other.

"Where's Gran and Bumps?" His eyes darted around nervously.

I laughed. "They are at church. They wanted to give us some privacy."

He waggled his eyebrows. "Oh really?"

I put my finger on his chest and shook my head. "Not that much privacy. Come on inside. Dinner is ready."

He stepped inside and closed the door behind him. He smiled and inhaled deeply. "That smells heavenly."

"Good. I made pork chops, mashed potatoes and gravy, green beans, and cornbread."

He looked at me and sighed heavily. "Sweeter words have never been spoken. I'm starving and haven't had anything to eat all day."

I grabbed his arm and pulled him into the kitchen. "Sit." I nodded at the small kitchen table and went to the stove to make him a plate. "Oh, and I made dessert too."

His eyes sparkled. "Well, don't make me guess. What did you make?"

I grinned. "Peach cobbler."

He bit his bottom lip. "My favorite. You didn't happen to make some homemade ice cream to go on top did you?"

I shook my head. "No. Bumps did." I sat his plate in front of him. He picked up his fork and started to stab a green bean.

I playfully slapped his hand. "Matthew, you haven't even said grace yet."

He set his fork down and gave me a pitiful look. "Sorry. It's just that I'm so hungry."

He waited patiently until I fixed my plate and sat down at

the table. He quickly folded his hands and said a quick prayer. As soon as he was done, he began to eat.

"This is so good." He said around a mouthful of potatoes.

I laughed and shook my head. "Thanks. Your mom told me how much you love steak but we didn't have that so I made pork chops instead."

He pointed his knife at the plate. "This is better than any steak I've ever had."

I shook my head. "I doubt that. You say that about everything I cook."

He shrugged. "It's true. You're a good cook. My mom never cooks and I think my dad's a bit jealous." He gave me a wink.

I warmed at the compliment. "Oh, I wanted to talk to you about the job offers I've gotten. I can't wait too much longer to commit someplace. There's a hospital near the seminary that I thought about taking. That way we could see each other more."

"Or we could just go ahead and get married." He looked at me.

I blinked. "But I thought you wanted to wait until we both graduated. You still have another year to go."

He set his fork and knife down and reached for my hands. "It's getting harder not to be with you all the time. I miss you, Kathleen. I feel like I'm lost when I'm not with you."

My heart fluttered at the sincerity in his eyes. I reached over and caressed his cheek. "I miss you too."

His eyes brightened. "So let's do it. Let's get married. Now."

I laughed. "Today?"

He frowned. "Well, not today, but within the next two weeks. We don't need a big wedding, right?"

Something in my chest tightened. I shook my head and

reminded myself not to be selfish. Gran said that the marriage was always more important than the actual wedding.

"I guess not." I smiled. "But how are we going to put a wedding together so soon? I don't even have a dress, or someone to marry us, or a venue."

He lifted his chin. "All we have to do is go to the court-house. A judge can marry us."

I pressed my hand to my chest. "Okay, and what am I supposed to wear? I need a dress."

"I bought you one. It's not a wedding dress but it's white and it will look great on you." He stood. "Wait here and I'll go get it."

Unease snaked through my gut. I felt like things were speeding up and I had no control over anything.

When he returned, he was carrying a white garment bag on a hanger. He held it out. "Here, go try it on."

I frowned. "I'm pretty sure you're not supposed to see me in my wedding dress."

He sighed heavily. "Then don't show me. Just go up and see if it fits."

I nodded as I took the bag. I climbed the steps with the garment bag, which felt like it weighed a hundred pounds.

I went to my room and closed the door behind me. I took a deep breath.

Since getting engaged to Matthew I had been dreaming and thinking of the details of my wedding. A spring wedding, a wedding dress with a white lace veil that I would pick out with Gran, a church wedding with everyone I had grown up with. It would be a day of joy.

Now I wouldn't even be married in the church I loved, invite my family and friends, or even pick out my wedding dress.

I hung up the dress and unzipped it. My stomach dropped. It was sleeveless with a sweetheart neckline. It was long and billowed on the sides with a large slit up the middle which would expose a lot of leg.

Reluctantly I undressed and slipped the dress on and looked in the mirror.

It was a beautiful dress, but it was clearly a cocktail dress, not a wedding dress. And it was not my style.

Resentment filled my heart.

I turned to take the dress off and my gaze landed on my bedside table where my worn Bible lay.

"Love is patient, love is kind. It does not envy, it does not boast, it is not proud. It does not

DISHONOR OTHERS, *it is not self-seeking, it is not easily angered, it keeps no record of wrongs. Love*

DOES NOT *delight in evil but rejoices with the truth. It always protects, always trusts, always*

HOPES, ALWAYS PERSEVERES." ~ *1 Corinthians 12:4-7.*

THOSE WORDS of what love really was rose up in my mind.

Self-seeking.

GUILT HIT ME HARD. That's what I was doing. Wanting a wedding exactly to my liking. Love didn't do that.

I blinked back tears as I shoved the dress off and hung it up.

I walked downstairs and met Matthew at the bottom step.

"Well?" he searched my face.

I forced a smile. "It fits perfectly. Looks like we'll be getting married in two weeks."

CHAPTER 17

The days leading up to the wedding were not exactly full of joy and excitement. Instead it was stressful and overwhelming.

I was ready for the wedding day to be over before it even started.

Bumps was heartbroken that he wouldn't be walking me down the aisle and Gran was upset that I wouldn't be getting married in our church.

Even worse was the guilt I felt. I had let them down by proceeding with this wedding so fast.

By the time we arrived at the courthouse, Matthew and his parents, Kitty and Jack, were there waiting. Aunt Kim, Uncle John, and Lori didn't come because they were on vacation in Europe and would not be back for another week.

Kitty, who was usually loving and doting, was cool and grim faced on this happy day.

Matthew's face lit up when he saw me and quickly herded everyone inside. He had the paperwork and seemed to ignore any questions that my Gran asked.

I thought we would have more time before we were

called up before the judge, but apparently we were the first ones to get married that day.

Butterflies filled my stomach and I wished I had eaten breakfast that morning. But I had been too nervous to keep anything down.

I was more anxious than I thought I would be. But then again, I'd never been married before. Maybe all brides felt this way.

As we walked up to stand before the judge, the door of the courtroom slammed, making me jump.

I turned around and froze.

Deacon Wilson was standing in the back of the room in slacks and a white button-up shirt.

The expression on his face was utter contempt for me.

I turned around to face the judge and almost jumped when Matthew took my hand in his. He gave me a reassuring smile. I held my breath waiting for Deacon to start some trouble on my wedding day.

I took a deep breath and listened as the judge spoke. When it came time to say our vows, my voice was sure and steady.

Once we were pronounced husband and wife, Matthew gave me a quick kiss and hugged me tight. I glanced over his shoulder to see Deacon leaving the courtroom.

Relief spread over me. I saw the man who made my life miserable, disappear once and for all.

CHAPTER 18

*A*fter our wedding we spent our honeymoon night at the Four Seasons in Atlanta, which Matthew's parents had paid for. We arrived at the hotel after dark, had a quiet dinner and then went back to our room.

I was so nervous. But as soon as Matthew kissed me, all my fear melted away. He was tender and gentle, and I knew our first time making love would be burned into my memory forever. Afterward as I drifted off to sleep in his arms, I felt at peace.

The next morning I awoke to an empty bed. Sitting up I surveyed the room and spotted Matthew's suitcase sitting in the corner.

I stretched and then crawled out of bed. The door opened and Matthew was standing there with two cups of coffee. His gaze landed on me and he smiled.

"I thought I'd run down and grab us some coffee before you got up. I was going to surprise you." He set the coffee down on the table and pulled me in for a kiss.

I melted against the warmth of his body and locked my fingers around his neck.

The kiss turned passionate and soon we were falling back into bed.

I put my hand on his chest and glanced up at him. "What time do we have to leave?"

A slow grin crossed his face. "We have time. Trust me." His lips covered mine and time seemed to evaporate.

A few short hours later we had checked out and were back on the road headed to Matthew's seminary.

"I don't think they'll let me live in the dorm with you, Matthew." I gave him a worried look.

He let out a laugh. "I wasn't planning on staying in the dorm. They have housing for married couples. We might have to stay off campus at a hotel until we get the house, but it shouldn't take too long." He reached for my hand and gave me a reassuring squeeze.

I nodded. I hadn't packed a lot of clothing because it had all seemed so rushed. Gran helped make sure I had my necessary clothing as well as a quilt she'd made for me. It was a double wedding ring quilt made with the prettiest pink and red floral pattern. She told me she made it a while back and had put it away until my wedding day.

It brought tears to my eyes when I saw how beautiful it was.

We made it back to the seminary after four hours of driving. Matthew had checked us into a Holiday Inn for the week. While it was no Four Seasons, it was clean and safe and would do until we got housing. I'd brought my laptop so I could look at my job options.

That night after grabbing a quick dinner of burgers and fries, we hurried back to our hotel room and began our life as Mr. and Mrs. Hollings.

CHAPTER 19

he week passed slowly at the hotel. Matthew would go to class early and get back sometime after six. He said this semester his classes were harder and he had to study at the library more than ever.

After graduating nursing school I completely understood. I quickly fell into a routine of grabbing the hotel's free breakfast before applying for nursing jobs online.

Since Matthew took my car to class, I was left without transportation which made it impossible for me to set up a time to interview. He told me not to worry and that his dad would be driving his car down to him soon.

Thursday morning when I went downstairs to grab some breakfast, Matthew was there talking to the receptionist at the front desk.

"Hey, I thought you would be in class." I blinked.

He reached for my hand and smiled. "I have great news to share."

I smiled. "We have a house?"

"Better. The school is going to move my classes to online.

Which means you can accept that job in Atlanta." His eyes brightened.

"Wait. Atlanta? I had other offers that are closer to Bumps and Gran that I was looking into. I never wanted to take the job in Atlanta."

He pulled me into his embrace. "I know sweetheart, but Atlanta's hospital is better. I've looked online at the benefits and it looks great. Also a lot of opportunity to move up and grow within the hospital."

I shook my head. "But even if you do online classes, won't you still have to go to class to take your tests?"

"Yes, and they are few and far between. Look, I know this isn't ideal, but there is no housing available and it doesn't look like we can stay in the hotel forever. Atlanta is a better option."

I frowned. "But we don't have a place to live in Atlanta."

His smile grew. "We do now. Mom and Dad are letting us stay at their townhouse in Buckhead. They only ever use it when they're in Georgia. Mom's gotten pretty fond of their house in California so they plan on moving out there permanently."

I gaped. "I didn't know they had more than one house." They were richer than I thought.

He blinked. "They actually have three. There's one in Wyoming where we go skiing." He shrugged. "Anyway, how exciting is this? We already have a house to call our own. Now go ahead and run upstairs to get packed. We are moving in today."

He turned back to the receptionist to finish checking out, leaving me standing there with my mind reeling.

With Matthew, I was learning things moved fast. Faster than I was ever used to .

CHAPTER 20

*W*e pulled up to the gated entrance and Matthew typed in the security code.

"I didn't realize it was a gated community." I gawked. "How long have your parents lived in this house?"

"About five years. They sold the big house after I graduated and wanted to downsize."

I blinked when we pulled up to what Matthew considered downsizing. The outside of the townhouse was timber and stone. There were at least three floors that I could see and it looked like it was pretty large for a townhouse.

A familiar car pulled up beside us and Matthew waved. "It's Mom and Dad. Mom wanted to give you the tour of everything."

I nodded and we got out of the car. Kitty pulled me into a hug the moment she saw me, seeming to be more affectionate than at the wedding. I chalked up her distance at the wedding, to her being hurt that we had a simple wedding, verses an expensive one where she could invite all her friends.

"Hi, Kitty. I can't thank you enough for letting us stay at your home." I smiled.

"Oh, hon, call me Mom." She gave me another quick hug. "Come on inside and let me show you around. I think it will be the perfect place for you and Matthew to start your life together."

I glanced over at Matthew and his father who had their heads together chatting about something.

As I followed Kitty into the house, I commented on all the flowers in her flowerbeds.

"Kathleen, you certainly know your flowers." Kitty gave me an impressed look.

I shrugged. "I guess I get it from my Gran. She had a ton of flowers, not to mention a vegetable garden."

Kitty nodded. "I wish I had more room for a garden here. That's what I love about the California house. Tons of space for my very own vegetable garden. I think it's important to eat as healthy as possible, especially at my age." She gave a self-deprecating laugh.

"I don't know what you mean. You look stunning. You look like you are thirty-five."

Kitty's face lit up with the compliment. She would never admit it but Matthew had told me she kept her plastic surgeon in his multi-million dollar house.

"Matthew tells me you are going to be working at the hospital here. Traffic gets kind of crazy so be sure to leave earlier if you anticipate getting there on time." Kitty stepped inside the front door. I followed.

My mouth dropped at the luxurious home. "It's huge. I thought townhomes were small."

Kitty laughed. "They can be. But in this neighborhood they are all thirty-five hundred square feet."

"I hope I can keep it clean." I blinked.

Kitty grabbed my arm and led me further into the house.

The living room was done in cool colors of grays and whites with a stone fireplace. The tall windows looked out over the treetops and there were French doors leading out to a balcony. The kitchen was beautiful and spacious. White cabinets and white quartz countertops gave the space a modern but warm feel. The floors throughout the house were hardwood and I noticed that Kitty had kept the walls a nice neutral color which made all her art hanging on the wall pop.

There were three bedrooms on the second floor and the master had its own fireplace and sitting area. The home office was located on the third floor and was minimalist in style.

After climbing down the stairs, we made our way back to the kitchen. "Well, Kathleen, what do you think?"

I gave my mother-in-law a big smile. "It's stunning. I can't imagine a more beautiful home for me and Matthew to start our married life. I can't tell you how much we appreciate this opportunity."

Kitty gave me a genuine smile. "Of course, sweetheart. That's what family is for. Supporting one another. Now let's go find the men and we'll take the happy couple out to our favorite restaurant."

As I followed after Kitty, my heart began to expand with joy and I sent up a prayer to God for all he had done in our lives to bring us to this moment in time.

CHAPTER 21

J quickly found a job at one of Atlanta's largest hospitals. I wanted a day shift position but I had to settle for working 11 a.m. to 7 p.m. on the medical surgical floor. It would mean getting home late to Matthew but he said he understood, and it would give him more time to do his classes online. That shift also paid a little more which I was grateful for.

Kitty and Jack had taken all of the art with them when they moved to California. Lucky for us, they left the furniture, otherwise we would be sleeping on the floor.

We soon fell into a schedule. I went to work. When I got home, Matthew would attempt to cook dinner or we'd order in. Matthew wasn't a cook so we ended up ordering pizza a lot. When I realized how much money we were wasting by ordering so much takeout, I began cooking meals on my days off so we could have something to eat throughout the week.

Today was my day off and I was finally finished cooking for the week. I set aside meatloaf for dinner. Matthew loved my meatloaf and he had complained that we hadn't had it in a while.

I went to the pantry and pulled out some potatoes. I'd make twice-baked potatoes and add a nice salad.

I smiled as I looked around the kitchen. It was nice to have a beautiful kitchen to cook in. I couldn't wait until Gran and Bumps could visit. Just thinking of them made my heart hurt. I really missed them and hadn't seen them since we moved to Atlanta.

I picked up my phone and pulled up Gran's number.

The phone rang four times before Bumps answered. "Hello?"

"Hey, Bumps." I smiled at the sound of his voice.

"Kathleen, hey, pumpkin. How are things going? We've really missed you."

I walked over to the balcony and stepped outside. "I know. I've missed you both too. I've just been crazy busy with my schedule. It seems by the time I get home, I only have time to make dinner and go to bed, only for it to start again."

Bumps let out a chuckle. "That's life, honey. You still like your job?"

I smiled and nodded. "Oh, yes. My nurse manager told me I'm next on the list to get a seven to three position. I figure once I get that, things will seem more regular and I'll get to see more of Matthew."

I heard a familiar voice in the background asking who Bumps was talking to.

"Is that Gran?" I asked.

"Of course. She just got in from the doctor's office."

I stiffened. "Everything okay?"

Bumps was mumbling something to Gran and I couldn't make out what they were saying.

"Here's your grandmother, honey. I love you." Bumps voice grew heavy with emotion.

"I love you too, Bumps. I'll come see you real soon."

I quickly calculated the next weekend I had off. I didn't remember seeing any free weekends, but I did have three days off in a row that I could make work.

"Kathleen?"

I smiled at the sound of her voice. "Hello, Gran. You giving Bumps a hard time since I've been gone?"

She huffed. "He's lucky I'm here to keep him straight."

I laughed at her joke.

"When are you coming home for a visit?" Gran asked.

I nodded. "I was just thinking about coming back on my days off."

"Good, good. We miss you around this old house. It's nothing like your fancy house…"

"The farmhouse is always home." I meant it.

"Tell me about work."

Soon we had settled into a conversation about how my work day normally went and the different kinds of patients I had taken care of so far. It was then I realized Gran had driven the conversation to take the focus off her.

"Hey, Bumps said you just got back from the doctor. Is everything okay?"

She let out a laugh. "Of course it is. He says my blood pressure is high so he is putting me on some medication. I guess my age is finally catching up with me."

Her words eased my mind. I glanced at the time on my watch and sighed. "I guess I need to go finish making dinner. Matthew should be home anytime now."

"Okay, honey. Let me know what day you are coming and I'll cook the fatted calf."

I laughed and we said our goodbyes and hung up.

As I went inside, I couldn't stop the ache in my chest. I missed my grandparents terribly, but I knew I would see them soon.

As I went about finishing dinner, I started planning how long it would take me to get back home.

CHAPTER 22

A week after talking to Gran, I was pulling into the driveway of the place I'd always called home. Matthew stayed in Atlanta because he still had schoolwork but told me to go ahead and visit my grandparents.

I smiled as I got out of my car and saw Gran opening the front door.

She hobbled down the steps of the front porch.

I left my bag and purse in the car and ran to her. I threw my arms around her neck, hugging her tightly.

"It's so good to see you. I missed you so much." She laughed.

"I missed you too, Gran." I pulled back and looked at her. She seemed thinner to me, a little more fragile. It made me sad to see Gran getting older.

"Bumps is in the barn. Go say hi and come back inside. I made your favorite chocolate chip cookies. And you can tell me about all the wonderful meals you are cooking that new husband of yours."

I nodded. "Sounds lovely."

I walked in the direction of the faded red barn. When I

was little I remembered Bumps getting some friends together to paint the barn every three years. It was kind of a big deal in our small community and afterward there was always a big BBQ meal with all the fixings.

It had been quite a few years since the barn had a fresh coat of paint. It was just one more reminder that nothing lasts forever.

I stepped inside the barn and stopped when I heard voices.

Bumps raised his voice. "You don't know what you are talking about."

I stiffened. For as long as I had known Bumps, he had never raised his voice to anyone in his life.

Feeling like an intruder, I started to back out when someone I recognized stepped out of the shadows.

Deacon Wilson.

He turned and glared at Bumps. "You better do something about it or I will."

Bumps pointed his finger in Deacon's chest. "You won't do anything, understand?"

Fear crawled up my spine. I stepped out of the shadows before I could stop myself. "Bumps, is everything okay?"

Bumps jerked his head in my direction and shuttered his expression. Surprise melted into delight at seeing me. He held out his arms and I went to him. "Kathleen, I'm so glad you're back."

I pulled back from the embrace and looked up at him. "Me too, Bumps." I glanced over at Deacon who glanced at me and then gave me his back.

"Gran has some cookies. Want to come with me?" I completely ignored Deacon. After what I heard in the barn, I wasn't inviting him inside.

And I was having a serious conversation with my grandparents about him.

"I'll be right in, Pumpkin." He gave me a bright smile.

I wasn't fooled. I could still see the worry behind his eyes.

I nodded. "Don't be too long." I glanced at Deacon who was now staring hard at me before heading back toward the house.

The screen door slammed behind me as I stepped inside. Gran poked her head out of the kitchen. "I made us some lemonade too. It's too hot for coffee."

I smiled and headed into the kitchen. I glanced around. Everything was the same. The same linoleum floor, the same butcher block countertops, the same old wall clock that struck every hour.

Yet something had changed. I could feel it.

I sat at the kitchen table and plucked a large chocolate chip cookie from the platter. The first bite melted in my mouth.

"Hmmm. Gran, your cookie recipe gets better every time I taste them." I closed my eyes and sighed.

She laughed and took a cookie for herself. "It's the same recipe we always made. Maybe just being home makes it taste better."

I smiled and contemplated how to broach the subject of Deacon. I figured there was no way to approach the subject delicately. "I saw Bumps in the barn. With Deacon."

Gran nodded. "He's helping around the farm this year."

I set my cookie down. "They were arguing. I didn't like the way Deacon was talking to Bumps."

A look of surprise flickered across Gran's face. "Arguing? I can't imagine about what."

I snorted. "You don't know Deacon like I do. I'm not so sure you guys should keep him on. He tends to have a temper."

Gran cocked her head at me. "Has he ever had a temper with you?"

I thought about it for a while. "Well, no. But in high school, he always got in trouble."

She didn't say anything for a moment and then looked at me. "I'll take into consideration what you said. I'll have a talk with Bumps and see what he thinks."

I nodded. "Good. I would feel a lot better knowing he wasn't around you two."

Gran smiled and patted my hand. "Now tell me all about what you and Matthew have been up to."

For the next hour we chatted happily about my new life in Atlanta, Matthew's online classes, and our plans for the future.

I looked out the back door and realized that I couldn't wait to see what great things happened next in our lives.

CHAPTER 23

*A*fter a year went by, I'd gotten moved to the day shift that I had requested. I was home early enough to clean up a bit before starting dinner. I thought that I would see Matthew more by getting home around four, but he was usually gone to the library when I got home. He'd get back just in time to eat around seven.

I was busy folding laundry when I heard Matthew come in.

"Kathleen? Where are you?"

I poked my head out of the laundry room. "I'm folding laundry." I was surprised how much laundry just the two of us could go through in a week.

He came around the corner and picked me up in his arms. "I've got some great news to tell you."

I kissed him and smiled. "What is it?"

He pulled back and looked down in my eyes. "I have a job offer. At a church near Augusta."

I blinked. "A job offer? Already? I mean you're not finished with seminary."

He gave me an easy smile. "That's the beauty of this job offer. They are going to hire me before I get out of school. They are desperate for a pastor at this small church and it would be a great opportunity."

I nodded. "I know but Augusta is hours away, which means I would have to find another job."

He laughed. "You won't have a problem getting another job. Nursing jobs are always available. And it might even pay more." He looked at me, waiting for my reaction.

"But where would we live?" I swallowed hard.

His smile widened. "We would live in the parsonage by the church. Which means rent free."

I frowned. "What kind of church is this?"

"It's the Chapel Baptist Church of Augusta. It's small which is good since it would be my first church. I'm telling you, Kathleen. It's like it was sent from God Himself." He lifted his chin.

I smiled, not wanting to rain on his parade and remembering that love was not selfish.

"It's wonderful, Matthew. And you're right. I'll be able to find another job at the hospital there."

He hugged me tight. "I knew you would be so happy. We are finally getting our own place and making our own path in life."

I frowned . "What about this house? What will your parents say? Won't they be upset that we are leaving it?"

He shrugged. "I'm sure it will be fine. Now go get dressed. I'm taking you out to dinner to celebrate."

That night as I was putting on my black dress that I only wore for special occasions, I sent up a prayer for God to make me more supportive of Matthew's dreams and less selfish.

By the end of the night, I was looking at things through Matthew's eyes.

My selfishness had melted away, replaced with gratitude that God had provided a church for my husband.

CHAPTER 24

"We are so happy to have you and your husband Matthew at Chapel Baptist Church. We've been trying to get a pastor for so long and then Matthew came across our radar." Mrs. Green smiled as she pulled out the keys to the parsonage. She was an older lady with gray hair and kind eyes. Her white dress with tiny yellow flowers ruffled in the breeze. She tapped her black clad shoe impatiently as she tried to figure out which key matched the front door lock.

"Thank you, Mrs. Green. I'm excited to see what God is going to do with us here." I smiled and looked at the tiny white house with two window boxes of withering purple petunias. I would have to water them later this afternoon after the harsh sun went down.

Mrs. Green stuck the key in the door and turned the knob. She stepped in first while I followed behind.

The living room was small with an old blue and red plaid couch, and two wooden rocking chairs that looked like they'd seen better days. There were two end tables which had been painted black and a matching coffee table.

"The ladies in the church came over and did a deep cleaning of the house. It's been vacant for almost a year." Mrs. Green headed to the kitchen. "The appliances are a bit dated but everything is in working order." She patted the cream-colored tile countertop and glanced around at the cabinets that had been painted a soft green color. The white and black linoleum floor glowed under a glaze of fresh polish.

I stepped over to the sink and looked out the window. "This is pretty. The backyard looks big."

She preened under the praise. "Oh it is. There's a deck leading out the back door and some flowers planted along the fence. If you have a dog, it's a good place to let him run."

I smiled sadly. "We don't have a dog. At least not yet. Maybe after we get settled."

Mrs. Green waved her hand toward a doorway that led out into the hallway. "Let's go see the bedrooms. There are two. The master is small and there's no en suite bathroom. But it's just outside in the hall. The other bedroom is small with no connecting bath. The second bathroom is on the other side of the house where the laundry room is located."

I nodded as she opened the bedroom door and stepped inside. There were only two windows, one facing the backyard and a small closet. The bed itself was a queen with only one nightstand and a chest of drawers.

I smiled. "I think this will do fine. Once I add some curtains and some pictures, it will be cozy."

Mrs. Green nodded. "That's what I think too." She headed to the bathroom, opening the door for me to step inside. It was a full bath with a tub and no separate shower. The toilet wasn't separate like Matthew's parent's house.

After showing me the rest of the house, we stepped into the backyard. The deck was old and needed staining but there was a pretty swing sitting under a canopy of limbs which made me smile. It reminded me of Gran and Bumps and sitting in the swing on the porch when I was a little girl.

"You like the swing, I see." Mrs. Green said.

"I do. Brings back a lot of childhood memories," I admitted. "It's a very charming house."

"Good. I'm glad you both are here. It's hard to find and keep a pastor here in Augusta. Our last pastor left for greener pastures in Atlanta. Said our church was too small and he needed one where he could minister to a lot of people."

I frowned. "I see."

"What I'm getting at, is I hope you and Matthew will be happy here and stay here for a very long time."

I smiled. "I'm looking to finally be settled in one place. To be honest, Atlanta was too big for my liking. I like a smaller setting and want to be in a church that feels like family. The church we attended in Atlanta seemed to be more concerned with building more numbers and not ministering to the needs already in the church."

Mrs. Green nodded sadly. "I'm afraid that's what's happening all around. It's just the times we are living in."

"Well, let's hope that's not the case here at Chapel Baptist Church. I hope we can be a shining light in the world."

Mrs. Green patted my hand and looked at me. Her eyes were misty with unshed tears. "I feel like you and Matthew are truly a miracle from God. We are so thankful and grateful you are both here."

I smiled. "Thank you for saying that. I was a little concerned at first because it was so last minute. But after our conversation, I have to say, you have put my mind at ease. Thank you so much for that, Mrs. Green. I guess I just have to trust where God leads."

Mrs. Green smiled, and nodded her head. "Amen to that."

CHAPTER 25

$\mathcal{W}$e moved into the parsonage on a Tuesday. Matthew had to preach that Sunday. He was nervous and really wanted to do a good job on his sermon so he spent much of the week in the church office to prepare. That left me alone to unpack and get settled.

I had put in some applications at two of the hospitals in Augusta. I tried not to worry about hearing back so soon so I threw myself into getting our new house ready.

I had gotten up early and showered before making Matthew a breakfast of eggs, bacon, toast, and grits. After breakfast he walked over to the church to his new office where I was left to sort through the boxes.

I propped my hands on my hips and looked around the living room. It was a sea of boxes among the modest furniture. I pulled my long hair up in a ponytail and got busy opening boxes. I had gotten so absorbed in putting things away that I lost track of time. Before I knew it, the front door opened and Matthew bounded inside.

"Hello, beautiful." He pulled me into a big hug.

I laughed as he kissed me. "Hello, yourself. Back so soon?"

He frowned. "Soon? It's almost one."

I blinked. "One? You're kidding?"

He laughed. "No. I'm guessing you didn't have time to make lunch. Don't worry. We'll go to this little diner that Mr. Green was telling me about."

I glanced at the empty boxes. "That sounds great. I got a lot done this morning. I hope to have everything put away by tomorrow."

He took my hand in his. "Great. Now go change and we'll go grab a late lunch."

Twenty minutes later we were pulling up to a small diner on the outskirts of town. The parking lot wasn't full and we guessed the lunch crowd had dispersed.

We were quickly seated in a booth with a red and white clad table.

A young blonde waitress hurried over to our table. "Hi, I'm Lorna. Can I get you two started with some drinks?"

I smiled. "I'll just have water."

Matthew looked up at her. "I'll have tea."

She wrote it down on her pad. "We have some specials for the day. Roast beef sandwich with a side of sweet potato fries. We also have a double cheeseburger with home fries. And if you are looking for something healthy we have a Cobb salad."

Matthew smiled and I noticed the young waitress blushing. Matthew tended to have that effect on young girls. They couldn't help but notice his good looks.

Matthew looked up at Lorna. "I think I'll have the double cheeseburger. What about you, Kathleen?"

I looked at Lorna. "Tell me, is the roast beef sandwich really good?"

Lorna's eyes widened. "Oh yes. It's my favorite on the menu."

I nodded. "Good, then that's what I'll have."

Lorna nodded, scribbled on her pad, then headed back to the kitchen. A few minutes later she returned with our drinks before waiting on a new customer.

Matthew reached for my hand. "I got a lot done today."

I brightened. "Really? That's great. Does that mean you'll be home for the rest of the day?"

He kissed the back of my hand. "Yes it does. Which means you'll need all your strength when we get back home."

I blushed at his words. It always amazed me how much he loved me. In the times when I didn't see him enough due to his classes, it was days like this when I was reminded of his affection.

And it was in these moments I knew how blessed I truly was.

CHAPTER 26

*J*held my breath as Matthew started his sermon that Sunday morning. He'd gone over to the church hours before the service was to begin. He said he wanted to be prepared and wanted his first sermon to be a good one.

I wore a cream-colored dress with a matching belt and black heels. I grabbed my worn Bible and my purse and headed over to the church.

"Good morning, everyone." Matthew smiled at the congregation.

The congregation greeted him warmly. The church itself was small but every pew held a group of members. There were a couple of young married couples with children and only a few young singles. But the majority of the members were made up of older, retired people.

Matthew launched into a sermon about loving thy neighbor. He gave some modern day examples of what that looked like and how we should be more like that in our daily lives. After he finished, he closed the sermon with a prayer.

Matthew walked down the aisle and waited for me to

stand. I walked hand in hand with him to the front door where he would say goodbye to his new parishioners.

"Pastor Hollings, that was a great sermon. I would have figured you might go over time, but you didn't." Mr. Green smiled.

"I didn't want to hold anyone hostage at my first sermon. It might scare some people away," Matthew joked as he shook the old man's hand.

"Kathleen, if there is anything you need, anything at all, please don't hesitate to ask." Mrs. Green smiled.

I nodded. "Thank you, that's very kind of you."

"Oh, I meant to tell you there is a women's Bible study on Wednesday at ten. We meet in the Fellowship Hall of the church. Everyone brings a dish to share after the study."

"Oh, I'm afraid I can't meet this Wednesday. I have an interview at the hospital at that time. But I will keep it in mind for the following week."

Mrs. Green didn't bother hiding the look of surprise that crossed her face. "Oh, I didn't realize you intended to work while Matthew is pastoring the church."

I nodded. "I hope to get a day shift so I can still be present to help at church with all the activities."

Mrs. Green relaxed and nodded. "I'm sure it will all work out."

About twenty-five minutes later, after the last member of the church left, Matthew shut the church door and looked at me.

"Kathleen, so tell me. What did you think about the sermon?" He held both of my hands in his.

I smiled. "I thought it was wonderful. Very to the point. A lot of pastors try to use a bunch of words that people don't understand."

He cocked his head and cringed. "Do you think it was too simple?"

I shook my head and took his face between my hands. "No sweetheart. It was perfect."

Relief crossed his features. "Good. I wanted to make a good impression and I want people to see me as approachable."

I nodded. "You definitely came across as approachable. You were perfect."

He grinned as he pulled me into a hug. "No one is perfect, Kathleen, but thanks for the unwavering support."

He pulled back and sighed. "Now what's for lunch? I'm starved."

"Good. Because there is a roast and potatoes in the crockpot just waiting for you."

As we walked back to our tiny house, my heart was full.

CHAPTER 27

I bounded into the office of the church. Matthew jerked his head up from his laptop computer.

"Guess what?" I beamed with excitement.

"What?" he stood from behind the desk.

"I got the job."

He came around the desk and pulled me into a hug. "I had no doubt. What will your schedule be?"

I lifted my chin. "That's the best part. I got a day shift, so it's seven to three, off on the weekends."

He looked shocked. "Off every weekend? That's practically unheard of in the medical world."

I nodded. "I know. It seems like one of the members of church is related to the nurse manager I interviewed with, and they knew I would prefer to have my weekends off to support my husband. Seems like you already have some pull."

He nodded approvingly. "Good to know." He tapped a finger on his desk on a piece of paper. "I almost forgot. I have something for you."

He plucked the piece of paper off the desk and handed it to me. "It's a schedule of the women's activities coming up and thankfully the majority of them take place on Saturday so you can attend."

I took the paper and nodded. "Perfect. My presumed start day is in two weeks so I can jump right in with these activities."

He smiled. "I'm sure Mrs. Green will love it if you give her a call. Her number is at the bottom of the paper."

I nodded and looked up at him. "Want me to bring you a sandwich?"

He shook his head. "Nah, I have a lunch appointment with the deacons. They are treating me to lunch at that diner we went to." He checked his watch. "Actually I should be heading over there now."

I smiled, glad he had been so welcomed to the small church. "I won't keep you. I was thinking pork chops for dinner?"

He gave me a quick kiss. "Sounds wonderful."

The second I got back to the house, my phone rang. I answered without looking at the caller.

"Hello?"

"Mrs. Hollings?" The woman's voice on the other end seemed slightly familiar.

"Yes?"

"This is Mrs. Collins. I came over with Mrs. Green last week and dropped off that pound cake."

I smiled. "Oh yes. Mrs. Collins. I have to tell you we enjoyed that cake. You'll have to give me that recipe."

The older woman laughed. "I hate to tell you, but that is a closely guarded family recipe. I don't give that recipe out to anyone. Not even to my best friend. But I will promise to make it again for you two sometime soon."

I chuckled. "That's very generous of you. I know you didn't call to talk about cakes. What can I do for you, Mrs. Collins?" I sat on the couch.

"We have our monthly Women's Missionary meeting this Saturday. We hold it on the first Saturday of every month and have a speaker. Afterward we have a potluck. This Saturday we have a retired missionary from Africa as our speaker. We usually do a gift bag as well as a monetary gift. We were wondering if you would like to shop for the gift?"

I nodded. "Of course. I can shop this afternoon if that's okay?"

Mrs. Collins squealed with delight. "That would be perfect. We usually stick to a fifty dollar limit on the contents of the gift bag and then we take up money before the speaker gets there on Saturday for the love offering."

I nodded. "Great I can't wait to attend. It will also give me a chance to get to know the women better. Thank you for asking me, Mrs. Collins."

"Of course, Mrs. Hollings. I just know you and your husband are going to be a great influence on our community."

After I ended the call with Mrs. Collins I pulled my Bible off the coffee table and turned to the book of Jeremiah, to my favorite verse.

"I know the plans I have for you, declares the Lord, plans for good and not for evil, to give you a future and a hope. ~Jeremiah 28:11"

I smiled as I closed the pages, meditating on the verse. God had certainly ordered our steps to this church and for a reason I didn't know.

One thing I did know. I would trust Him with my doubts and whatever else came next.

And in doing so, God would give me a wonderful future with my wonderful husband.

CHAPTER 28

"That was a wonderful speech you gave," I smiled at Mrs. Whitmore, the guest speaker. "I always found it fascinating to be a missionary in a foreign country. I'm afraid that I don't think I could go into a foreign land without a massive amount of fear and uncertainty."

Mrs. Whitmore laughed. "Oh, Mrs. Hollings, it's those valleys of uncertainty that we grow the most. Trust me. I know."

Mrs. Green walked over with a platter of fried apple pies. "May I offer either of you one of my famous apple pies?"

Mrs. Whitmore clasped her hands together. "How wonderful. My mom used to make these when I was a child. These look just like them. I bet they will taste just like them too." She took one and placed it on her plate.

Mrs. Green held out the platter to me. "Thank you. These look wonderful." I took one as well.

The second I bit into the fried apple pie, my childhood memories came flooding back. It made my heart ache and I wished Gran was here enjoying this moment with me.

"These are wonderful, Mrs. Green."

The older woman smiled and lifted her chin as she carried her platter to the next table.

Mrs. Whitmore placed her hand on my arm. "So you are the new pastor's wife. The other ladies told me this is his first position."

I nodded. "Yes. We are very pleased that he got this job here, especially since he's still taking seminary classes."

Mrs. Whitmore frowned. "He hasn't graduated seminary yet?"

I shook my head. "No. The church was in desperate need of a pastor and they knew he only had one more semester to go so they decided to go ahead and hire him."

Mrs. Whitmore cocked her head. "You know they sure do things differently than when I was a pastor's wife stateside. They used to send a committee to hear a pastor and they would decide whether or not he was to be called to pastor their church." She shrugged. "I guess that takes too long in this instant society."

Mrs. Green returned. "Mrs. Whitmore, I would love to introduce you to the ladies in the back."

Mrs. Whitmore smiled. "Of course." She stood and placed her napkin on the table. She looked at me. "It was a pleasure to meet you, Mrs. Hollings."

I nodded. "I'm really glad you could come to our meeting today. I hope you will consider coming back."

She smiled and nodded. "I just might do that." Mrs. Whitmore let Mrs. Green lead her to the group of women in the back of the fellowship hall.

That night while I was washing dishes, I looked over at Matthew. "Can I ask you something?"

"Sure." He put his phone down and gave me his full attention.

"Do you think it was unusual for this church to hire you without hearing you preach?"

He chuckled. "Not really. From what they said it sounded like they were in a bind so they were desperate to hire someone."

I nodded and focused my attention on washing dishes.

He walked over behind me, put his arms around my waist and pressed his lips to my neck. "Why are you asking? You sound worried."

I shook my head and shoved any lingering doubts away. "No. I guess I'm used to a small country church where things are done differently." I turned in his arms and put my soapy wet hands on either side of his face.

He grimaced and laughed. He swung me up in his arms and carried me back to our bedroom.

Any unease I had was quickly forgotten as I found myself in his arms.

CHAPTER 29

"Are you sure you and Bumps can't come? We'd love to have you and there's a guest bedroom at the parsonage." I glanced over at Matthew who was busy going through his sermon notes.

We'd been in Augusta for almost three months and had been quite busy. Between my shifts at the hospital and being involved in the church activities, I had not seen my grandparents in quite some time.

"It's just so busy here on the farm," Gran's voice wavered. "Your grandfather needs all the help he can get and I'm not as young as I used to be. We'd love to see you both when you get a free day."

My heart sank. "I know. It seems life is busy for everyone nowadays. I'm hoping once the holidays are over, things will settle down. I'm sorry that we won't be home for Christmas."

Gran sighed. "I know, honey. You're an adult now with adult responsibilities. Just know we love you, and try to come when you can."

After I ended the call my heart felt heavy. I missed my

grandparents like crazy. It made me sad that I wouldn't be seeing them over the holidays. I went into the living room and sat on the couch, staring at the artificial Christmas tree that I'd found in the storage room of the laundry room.

The decorations were a collaboration of cheap red and silver balls, homemade crocheted snowflakes, and some silver tinsel. It wasn't a pre-lit tree so I had to string the colored lights on the five foot tree. It wasn't a pretty tree by any means, but it was all we had and I was happy with it. The parsonage had also come with a manger scene with Mary, Joseph, and baby Jesus that we set up on the front lawn. Gran had sent two Christmas stockings with our names knitted on them. They were red and green. She'd sewn snowmen on the front. We didn't have a fireplace, so I hung them on a book-shelf near the tree.

I looked around the house at the festive decorations, and still felt a sense of longing.

Matthew stepped into the room. "What did your grand-parents say? Are they coming for Christmas?"

I shook my head. "No. Not this year." I cleared my throat. "What about your parents?"

Matthew's face grew strained as he shook his head. "No. They are spending it in California."

I frowned. "That's too bad. You know I really haven't heard from your mom in a while. She usually calls pretty frequently, but since we've moved to Augusta, I think she's only called a couple of times. Is everything okay with them?" I'd wanted to ask Matthew a while back, but every time I brought up his parents, he quickly changed the subject.

He blew out a breath. "I think my parents wanted me to be pastor of a bigger church."

I blinked. "What does it matter as long as you're preaching the message of Christ?"

Matthew sat down next to me and put his arm around my shoulder. "They just want to see me succeed, that's all. So what activities are planned for the church? It seems like after we had the hanging of the green, it seems to be something every weekend."

I nodded. "I have the cookie exchange with the ladies' Bible study group, and you have the pancake breakfast with the men's Bible study, this weekend. We have to do the fruit baskets for our elderly that are in the hospital and housebound. And the deadline for the donation to the children's orphanage is this Friday where people will drop off the requested Christmas gifts. Then there is the Carols and Candlelight on Christmas Eve service."

"Wow, that's a lot." Matthew snorted.

"January will slow down a lot. So we'll get a break." I stifled a yawn.

"We certainly deserve it." He stood up. "I've got to get back over to the church. The men are having another meeting. It may run late so don't wait up for me. Sounds like you need to go to bed early." He kissed my head and started for the door.

I propped my feet up on the couch and stared at the Christmas tree. This time of year was my favorite holiday, but this year, it felt different.

I wanted to call Gran back to chat some more, but I knew she was probably at her own church decorating it for Christmas. I knew how disappointed she was in us not coming home for the holidays. It would be the first holiday that I didn't spend at the farm. And Matthew was working more. He spent all his days in the office of the church or meetings with the deacons, only coming home for dinner. I had thought with this new pastorate job we'd have more time together, but that wasn't turning out to be true.

Then there was my schedule. Working Monday through Friday had taken a toll on some of the relationships with the women at the church. They often chided me for not being more available to them, which left me feeling guilty.

I'd often heard of people having the holiday blues and now that's what was happening to me.

I picked up my phone and dialed my cousin Lori. She picked up on the third ring.

"Lori, it's Kathleen." I smiled.

"Kathleen! Hey! I can't wait to see you at Christmas. So much has happened and I want to tell you everything." The excitement was evident in her voice.

My stomach dropped. "I'm sorry. I won't be able to come home for Christmas. Between my work schedule along with Matthew's schedule, we are crazy busy. But maybe after the holidays I can make a trip home."

Lori huffed. "I can't wait that long. Wait, I have an idea. I'm in Atlanta for a few days. What if I drive over tomorrow?"

My heart leapt in my chest. "Really? You'd drive over here?"

"Sure! It's not that far. I could be there around noon." Lori stated.

I nodded. "That would be perfect. We can have lunch here, I'll make lasagna and you can tell us all about your news."

Lori giggled. "That's perfect. Text me the directions."

I smiled and nodded. "I'll do it as soon as we hang up. And Lori?"

"Yes?"

"I'm really glad that I'll get to see you. I've missed you." I meant it. As different as we were, Lori was family and seeing her would make me less sad about the holidays.

When we ended the call, I quickly sent a text with directions, along with a picture of our house so she could easily find the right home.

Suddenly the holiday didn't seem so sad.

CHAPTER 30

"*W*ant some cake, Lori? One of the ladies from church dropped it off yesterday. It's home-made red velvet."

Lori's eyes went wide. "I'm stuffed from the lasagna, but I don't think I can turn down a piece of that."

I laughed and served up three pieces of cake for the table.

"How long are you here for?" Matthew asked before taking a bite of cake. He smiled, pointing to the red velvet slice with his fork and nodded his approval.

"I have to head back tonight. I'm still not finished Christmas shopping and Mom wants me to go with her tomorrow." She took a bite of the dessert and moaned. "This is wonderful. Better than Mom's. And you can never tell her."

I laughed. "I won't. So what's your big news?"

Lori set her fork down and looked between me and Matthew. "I got a job. A dream job actually. It's being an assistant to a really rich guy in California. His last assistant is a friend of mine and she's getting married and moving to France, so he needs someone." She sat back and waited for our reaction.

"Does it pay good?" Matthew arched his brow.

Lori smiled and nodded. "Six figures starting out plus an apartment near his house."

My mouth dropped. "Six figures. Wow, that's great!"

Lori clapped her hands together. "I know! And I'll be living by the beach, which is my dream while getting paid a ton by some old rich guy." She shrugged. "Who knows, maybe he'll fall in love with me and ask me to marry him."

I snorted. "Lori, you wouldn't marry someone you were not in love with."

She arched her brow. "I've been in love too many times. I don't believe in love any more. It never lasts. But money does."

Matthew barked out a laugh. "Not if you blow it, it doesn't."

Lori shrugged. "Anyway, I'm moving to California in January." She reached over and squeezed my hand. "I'm glad I got to see you before I leave."

I nodded. "Maybe we can come out and see you. I mean, Matthew's parents live in California."

"Oh yeah, what part?" Lori took another bite.

"Montecito." Matthew said before finishing off his cake.

Lori gasped. "You're kidding! That's where I'm moving."

My eyes widened. "Really. What a wonderful coincidence."

Matthew nodded. "Maybe we will have to make a trip out there. Who knows, maybe we can talk your grandparents into going with us."

That night as I lay in bed I was filled with a mix of emotions. I was sad but excited for Lori. It seemed like her dreams were finally coming true. I was grateful for Matthew's position at church and my job, but sad that it seemed that I was living my adult life without my grandparents to see all the great things that were happening for us.

As I drifted off to sleep, I wondered what else was about to change for us as well.

CHAPTER 31

"What do you have to tell me, Matthew?" I glanced around the expensive restaurant where he'd taken me for dinner. I'd even put on my most expensive dress for the occasion.

"I have something to tell you that you won't believe." Matthew took a sip of his tea.

I clasped my hands together. "Okay, but I have something to tell you too. I have some news of my own."

He blinked and cocked his head. "You go first."

I smiled. "I just got a raise at work. My nurse manager said she was very impressed with my work and recommended I get a raise. It was approved."

Matthew blinked. "Wow, that's great. And you've not even been there a year. Getting a raise is really big news. Congratulations, sweetheart."

I smiled, pleased with myself. "Thank you. Okay now you go. What's your big news?"

Matthew couldn't contain his excitement. "You're not going to believe this, but...I have been offered a position at a large church in California. They offered me three times what I am currently making."

The smile slid off my face. "California?"

He nodded. "Yes. Isn't it wonderful? We would be closer to my parents and Lori."

My stomach turned as my heart thudded in my chest. I didn't want to move to California. I wanted to stay right where we were.

"I thought you'd be excited." Matthew's expression shifted.

I shook my head. "I'm shocked. I mean, California is literally on the other side of the country. And so far away from my grandparents."

He nodded and looked down at his plate. "I know it's hard to think about moving away from everything you know, but change is good. You never know what this move will bring and how many lives I can change by preaching at a bigger church."

I swallowed hard. "Have you told our church about this?"

He shook his head. "No. I wanted to talk to you first. I plan on telling them tomorrow."

I looked up at him. "So you have already decided."

He sighed heavily. "Kathleen, there are some opportunities in life that you can't say no to. Think of the greater good. With a bigger church, we'll be able to expand my ministry and change lives. Now is not the time to be selfish."

Selfish. Was that what I was being? Selfish.

"What about my work?" I looked at him.

He cocked his head. "You always complain that we don't get to spend enough time together. There's a bonus to this move."

I frowned. "What's that?"

He took my hand in his. "With this job, you won't have to work."

I felt the blood drain from my face. "What?"

Matthew smiled. "You see with the amount of money I'll be making you won't have to work. You can help me at the church with the ministry. You won't ever miss out on any of the ladies' events again. I know that has bothered you. Now you won't have to worry."

I pulled my hand out of his. "But I love my job. I love being a nurse."

He nodded. "Look, we don't have to decide on anything right now. Once we get to California, and we see how the church is going, you can decide then. If you really miss it once we are all settled then you can go back to work."

His words made me feel a little bit better.

I looked up at him. "I feel really bad for all the members at our church. I feel like we are abandoning them."

He shook his head. "It's not like that at all. In fact, I'll make some suitable suggestions regarding my replacement. A few of the guys I went to school with are looking for a new opportunity."

Our dinner arrived and the conversation was over. I had lost my appetite but I made an effort since Matthew had taken me to such a nice restaurant. We hardly ever ate out and when we did it was something affordable. Now was not the time for me to get lost in my emotions. No matter how much I wanted to cry.

CHAPTER 32

"$\mathcal{M}$rs. Green, I can't tell you how much we will miss you and all the members of Chapel Baptist." I folded my hands in my lap and looked at the woman sitting at my kitchen table.

She shook her head. "I just don't understand. I thought Matthew would be pastoring us for at least three years. At least that's what the contract stated that he signed." She pressed her lips into a thin line.

I blinked. "Three years?"

She nodded furiously, obviously very put out at losing their pastor. "Yes. It was part of the agreement. He would preach three years and in turn the church would pay off any loans he had left in seminary."

I frowned and shook my head. "Mrs. Green, Matthew's parents paid for seminary. He didn't take out any loans."

She lifted her chin and froze me with a look. "Mrs. Hollings, I don't know what your husband told you but he took out student loans to go to seminary school." She stood quickly and hiked her purse up on her shoulder. "I don't get in other people's business, but if he were my husband, I

114

would have a talk with him about this." She headed for the door.

Shocked, I stood. My feet felt like concrete and I couldn't move. Why would Matthew lie about having his parents pay for seminary? What would be the point? It didn't make any sense.

Mrs. Green opened the door and cast a glance over her shoulder at me. "Perhaps it is for the best that you two leave. We don't tolerate wolves in sheep's clothing at our church." She closed the door behind her.

I stood there, rooted to the ground. Surely it couldn't be true. Matthew wouldn't lie to me about something like that. It didn't make any sense.

I went to my phone and dialed Matthew's number. He didn't answer and it went straight to voicemail.

I racked my mind with what Mrs. Green had said. Maybe she was mistaken. Maybe she had gotten something twisted. Maybe it was just a rumor that got started because the congregation was upset that they were leaving.

I couldn't blame them for that. I was upset as well. Despite trying to put on a brave face, I felt nauseated over the whole thing. I felt like my life was being uprooted to some foreign land that I knew nothing about.

I went into the living room with the phone in my hand to call Gran and Bumps. They were still unaware of our move. I wanted to tell them in person, not over the phone.

The front door swung open and Matthew burst through. He stopped when he saw me. "Kathleen. I thought you would be at work."

I shook my head. "I have the next few days off. After I told my boss about us moving she cut my hours. She said she needed to find someone dependable."

He nodded slowly.

I cleared my throat. "Matthew, Mrs. Green just left."

He cocked his head. "Mrs. Green? Did she drop off another one of her desserts?"

I slowly shook my head. "No. She came over here to tell me how disappointed she was in us leaving."

He shrugged. "That's expected. They were without a pastor for so long, they hate to have to go through the process of finding one all over again."

I stood and looked at him. "Matthew, that's not all she said."

He set his keys down on the coffee table and headed into the kitchen.

I followed.

He pulled a mug down from the cabinet and reached for the coffee pot. It would still be warm from breakfast. "Oh, yeah? What else did she say?"

I put my hand on his arm and he looked at me. "She said that us leaving so early goes against the contract you signed. She said the contract stated you would preach for three years in exchange for the church paying off your student loans."

He blinked and then turned his attention back to the coffee.

"Matthew, why didn't you tell me you took out student loans? You told me your parents were paying for seminary."

He sighed heavily and set his mug down. "I told you my parents were paying for law school. When I changed my career, they refused to pay for seminary."

I blinked and shook my head. "Why didn't you tell me? Since we are married, any student loan debt you take on becomes mine too."

He gave me a sad look. "Kathleen, is that really all you think about? Money?"

His words hit me like a ton of bricks. Anger flared inside me and I fisted my hands at my sides. "No, it's not. What I do think about is my husband being honest with me." I headed into the bedroom and slammed the door behind me.

Sitting on the bed, I contemplated what I should do next. Matthew opened the door.

I looked up at him. "How could you lie to me?"

He took a deep breath and walked further into the room. "Kathleen, if I had known this would make you so upset, I would have told you from the beginning. If it's the money you are worried about, then stop. Once we get to California, the church there will pay off my student loans."

He walked over and reached for my hand, pulling me to my feet. He brushed my hair away from my face. "Sweetheart, I'm sorry. I'm sorry I didn't tell you. As your husband, I just didn't want you to worry. I promise from here on out, I'll be totally honest about everything." He smiled at me.

I was still mad. I just wasn't sure how long I could stay mad at Matthew. He always had a way of putting things right.

I sighed. "I need to tell Gran and Bumps we are moving to California. I want to go tomorrow. There is no way I can tell them over the phone."

He nodded. "Of course. Do you want me to go with you? It will be good for me to get away. Maybe Bumps needs something that I can help with."

The sincerity in his eyes and the way he held me made me believe he was telling the truth.

I nodded slowly. "That would be nice if you went with me. They'll be glad to see you. It's been a while."

His grin widened. "Great. We'll start out early tomorrow and spend the night with them before heading home." He bent his head and kissed me in a way that reassured me everything would be alright.

CHAPTER 33

The look on Bumps and Gran's face almost broke my heart.

I swallowed hard. "It's not like it's on the other side of the world."

Gran nodded. "But it is on the other side of the United States. We'll never see you again, Kathleen."

Matthew stood and gave everyone a reassuring smile. "I know it sounds like it will be impossible to see Kathleen, but we will fly you both out there every other month if it will make things easier."

Gran frowned. "Flights cost a lot of money, Matthew. Not to mention me and Bumps have never flown before."

I walked over and sat down beside Gran. "I know, but this is a great opportunity for Matthew. He'll have a large congregation and his parents are out there. Not to mention that Lori will be out there as well. We could arrange your flights whenever Uncle John and Aunt Kim fly out to see Lori. That way you won't be alone when you fly and it won't be so difficult."

Bumps rubbed his chin in a thoughtful way. "Never been to California."

Matthew smiled. "I think you'll both love it. Weather is great and there's so much to see."

Gran reached for my hand. "Is this move going to make you happy, Kathleen?"

I blinked and then laughed. "I haven't thought about that. But I suppose it will make Matthew happy. So yes, it will make me happy."

Bumps looked over at me. "What about a job? Have you looked for nursing jobs yet?"

I looked from him to Matthew. I knew Matthew was just aching to tell Bumps I didn't have to work if I didn't want to. But for some reason I didn't want Bumps to know that.

I shook my head. "Not yet. But like we all know, there is no shortage of nursing jobs, so it should be fine. Besides, I hear nurses make a lot of money out there."

Gran stood. "I'll go fix us some lemonade."

I followed her into the kitchen. I watched quietly as she made the lemonade from scratch.

"Gran, I know you're upset…"

She spun around and looked at me. I saw the hurt in her eyes. "Kathleen, I'm not just upset, I'm hurt. Did you two know this was coming? Why are you springing it on us right now?"

I shook my head and sat down in the kitchen chair. I heard the front door slam and knew that Bumps and Matthew were walking outside. Bumps was probably showing him something in the barn. My grandfather always had some ongoing project in the barn.

I sighed heavily. "Gran, I just found out, a few days ago. You are just as shocked as I am."

She frowned. "Kathleen, is he making you do something you don't want to do?"

I grimaced. "Gran, he's my husband. How can I be a good wife to him, if I don't support his dreams?"

She snorted. "Marriage goes both ways, you know."

Her words struck something in my heart.

"Promise me that you and Bumps will come out to see us." I reached for her hand.

She looked at me for a few seconds before bobbing her head up and down. "Fine. I'll promise to come visit you. But I will probably be like a fish out of water the whole time."

That brought a smile to my face. "Then that will make two of us."

CHAPTER 34

"**W**e've heard great things about you, Pastor Hollings. And we are thrilled to have your lovely wife, Kathleen. We know she will be such a help here at Elate Church." Mrs. Winters, the wife of Mr. Winters, gave me a big smile. She was well over my age, but certainly didn't look it. It was obvious she had a lot of cosmetic procedures done.

I smiled. "Thank you, Mrs. Winters. Everyone has been very welcoming since we arrived yesterday. Another couple, I think it was the Belvederes, took us out for a wonderful dinner. They even picked us up from the hotel."

Mrs. Winters nodded. "Yes, Helen and I are great friends. She told me how delightful you both are." She craned her neck toward the front of the massive church. Matthew and her husband, William, were talking on the stage of the church. "I think William is showing Matthew the latest electronic equipment we just got. Some special effects for the praise worship."

I chuckled. "Sounds like a concert."

Mrs. Winters smiled. "The kids really love it. We do what we can to bring them in. There's so many other influences out in the world that we have to compete with." She looked back at her husband and nodded. "Let's go check out the rest of the church."

I followed her out of the enormous sanctuary and down a wide hallway.

"We have our adult classes on the second floor. This here is our children's wing. We have everything from the nursery all the way to eighth graders. We built another building to house our high school and college age kids. You probably saw it when you came into the parking lot."

I nodded. "Yes. It's very large."

Mrs. Winters lifted her chin. "We have the biggest college student attendance in the area."

I smiled. "That's wonderful. Are you doing a lot of mission trips for the students?"

She laughed. "Yes. We have students that volunteer every week at the local animal shelter. It's great for them to give back."

I blinked, trying to phrase my next question without offending her. "That's always good to give back. What about mission trips overseas?"

Her eyes grew wide. "Oh, no. It's too dangerous. You hear about all those kidnappings and worse." She stopped at a door and opened it. She flicked the light switch.

The room illuminated in light and I looked around the nursery. Bright cartoon characters were painted on the wall. There were ten rocking chairs and changing tables, along with diaper dispensers lining the wall.

"You guys must have a lot of volunteers to help out here. It's enormous." I looked around the room.

"We do." She replied happily. "Let's go upstairs and I'll

show you the adult groups classrooms. We'll swing by your husband's office first. We took the liberty to spruce it up a bit with some new artwork."

I nodded. "I can't wait to see it." In the back of my mind, I wondered what Mrs. Winters would think of the church we had left behind. This church was ten times bigger, newer, and more beautiful.

It felt too big.

I walked silently behind Mrs. Winters.

The woman stopped at a set of glass French doors and smiled at me. "I think you're going to really like how we decorated the office." She opened the door and walked in first.

I stepped inside something that looked like it came out of a designer magazine.

There was a small area where the secretary sat. Artwork hung on the walls. There was another door which led to Matthew's office.

We stepped inside and I glanced around.

Mrs. Winters looked at me intently. "Well, what do you think? We changed out the artwork for a local artist who sells really well. And the bookcases have been updated with a more expensive wood which looks more modern."

I shook my head. "It's really stunning. Looks like something out of a magazine."

Mrs. Winters clasped her hands together. "That's the response I was hoping for."

I nodded. "We've never had a church this. ... big before."

She smiled warmly. "Don't worry, dear. This is going to be a great experience for you both." She walked out of the office leaving me standing in the office alone.

Worrisome thoughts, along with regret, began to creep into my mind.

I began to second guess our move. Had we done the right thing? Or was this going to be a mistake?

I had an idea I was about to find out.

CHAPTER 35

It had been three months since we moved to California. Three months of me not working. Three months of me throwing myself into the church activities. Three months of Matthew preaching.

We had everything we could want. A beautiful home, new friends, and a successful career for Matthew.

Somehow I still felt empty.

I looked out the window over the kitchen sink into the beautifully manicured backyard. Today, however, was different. Today, I was picking up Gran and Bumps from the airport.

"You probably need to start out early. You know how traffic is." Matthew cast a glance at me over the rim of his coffee cup.

I nodded in agreement and washed out my cup before sticking it into the dishwasher.

"I was just about to head out. I put some meat in the refrigerator to thaw for dinner tonight."

Matthew shook his head. "No. We'll go out. I bet your

grandparents have never had an expensive meal in their life. It's good to splurge."

I cringed. "I don't know. I think they'll be tired from their trip. Why don't we just take them out to eat tomorrow?"

Matthew sighed heavily and stood. "Fine. Tomorrow it is." He looked at the time on his expensive watch that the church had gifted him. "I need to get going. I've got a men's meeting."

I frowned. "Will you be home afterward?"

He shook his head. "No, but I will try to leave work earlier than five today." He kissed the top of my head and headed out the front door.

I had thought that once we got here and I didn't have to work that we would have more time to spend together.

I was wrong. Matthew was always at the church. When he wasn't there, he was either playing golf with some of the members, or going over to his parent's house to help with something.

It left me with a lot of time on my hands. Two weeks ago I started looking into nursing jobs at the closest hospital, just to see what was available.

I grabbed my purse and headed out to my car.

Matthew had wanted me to buy a new car once we got here, but I was satisfied with my old car. He made me park it in the garage. He said it was to protect it from the elements, but I knew better. It was so the neighbors wouldn't see.

He'd bought a Mercedes the first week he started working. I was upset and told him we needed to be careful with our finances, but he wouldn't listen. He said that God had blessed him with this new job so he could be a blessing to others. He said he could not show up to church driving his old car.

We usually had dinner with his parents every Friday night. They seemed pleased that Matthew was doing so well

NOT LIKE THE OTHER GIRLS

in his career. With him making more money, I supposed they didn't mind him being a pastor.

As far as the student loans were concerned, I only brought it up once. He said the church had paid them off and for me not to worry.

I climbed into my car and eased out of the garage. Once I hit the highway, I let myself get excited about seeing Gran and Bumps again. It had felt like an eternity since we'd seen them.

I pulled up at the airport and waited my turn. I spotted Aunt Kim and Uncle John immediately and tried to catch their eye by waving out my window.

Uncle John's eyes widened when he spotted me and he waved back.

I pulled up to the curb and got out.

"Kathleen!" Aunt Kim smiled and ran over and hugged me. "You look wonderful. I see all this California sun makes you look like a million bucks."

I laughed. "Thanks." I looked over her shoulder. "Where's Gran and Bumps?"

She shook her head. "Still waiting on his luggage."

I frowned. "Why didn't they just carry on?"

She sighed a little. "They didn't want to keep up with the carry-on luggage between connecting flight, so they checked it. John is going back inside to see if he can speed things up."

I nodded as I went over to pop open my trunk.

Aunt Kim put her expensive luggage in and turned back. "I hope they hurry up. They only let you park here for so long."

Uncle John hurried out the door rolling three luggage bags.

Aunt Kim brightened. "Here they come." She ran over and helped with the luggage while Uncle John turned his attention to helping navigate Gran and Bumps who were trailing behind him.

I smiled and hurried over to them. Gran was wearing a scowl along with her green pantsuit that she usually reserved for Sunday church service. Bumps was looking around and trying to talk to the airport employees.

"Gran!" I held out my arms.

Her expression softened when she saw me and hugged me tight. "Kathleen. We finally made it. I can't believe how many people they cram into those seats."

I chuckled. "Yeah, well I guess everyone has to make a buck."

She snorted. "You don't say." She turned and waved Bumps over.

He spotted me and grinned. "Kathleen!" He pulled me into his arms and hugged me tight.

When he released me, I looked at both of them. "I'm so glad you are both here."

Aunt Kim patted me on the shoulder. "Kathleen, thanks for picking us up. Lori said she would pick us up from your house. She said her boss is running her ragged."

I arched my brow but didn't say anything.

Lori had told me she hardly did any work, and I wondered if she was having a romantic relationship with her employer. Whenever I tried to pry, Lori changed the subject, so I let it go. Instead I just prayed for her.

"No problem. Let's get these bags in the car and head out before we get caught in traffic."

My heart felt light as we drove away from the airport and headed back home.

CHAPTER 36

Gran had been quiet since she arrived at my house. She seemed reserved and not her usual joyful self. Bumps, on the other hand, went from room to room, marveling at everything from the size, to the expensive decorations, to how huge the refrigerator was.

Lori had come over after lunch to pick up her parents. Bumps went to lay down in their room for a nap. That left me and Gran alone in the living room.

"Would you like some more tea? I made it sweet, just like you like it."

Gran smiled and shook her head. "No. I have to watch my sugar intake these days."

I frowned. "Is anything wrong? Did the doctor say you were diabetic?"

Gran snorted. "No dear. I'm just getting old. That's all. I've got to stay healthy to take care of Bumps. That man would be lost without me."

I grinned. "We all would."

She stood to walk over to the large picture window and gazed out into the backyard. "Your house is huge, Kathleen. I wasn't expecting all this. Matthew must be making a ton of money." She turned to look at me.

"He makes really good money. And he's closer to his parents, which is what he wanted."

She smiled softly. "And what do you want, Kathleen? You're not even working."

I shrugged. "It's not like we need the money."

She frowned. "Nursing was never about the money, not for you. Tell me, are you happy?"

I didn't answer right away. I hadn't really thought about happiness, just trying to live a life that pleased God.

"Life is good, Gran. I have no reason to complain." I finally said.

She looked at me and gave me a sad grin. "I think I'll go take a nap with Bumps. I'm not used to the time difference."

I watched as she headed slowly to the guest room.

Heading into the kitchen, I pulled out my recipe book and got busy prepping for dinner. I needed something to occupy my mind and cooking always helped.

Hours later, the house smelled delightful. Proudly I put the last dish on the dining room table.

"Wow, Kathleen, this looks amazing." Bumps smiled.

"I think you've done too much, Kathleen. We would have been happy with just a sandwich," Gran stated.

Her words hurt, but I shoved my feelings away and laughed. "I can't have you coming all this way to California and give you a sandwich to eat."

Matthew nodded encouragingly, "Kathleen has been making more and more gourmet foods. Last week she even made a French dish which was marvelous."

Bumps grinned. "Looks like you have the best of both worlds, Matthew. A wonderful career and a wife who knows how to cook."

Matthew nodded in agreement.

Gran snorted.

"I like to think I'm more than just a cook," I muttered.

Gran looked at Matthew. "Tell me Matthew. How do you feel about Kathleen going back to nursing?"

Matthew passed the dishes after he served himself and gave my grandmother a warm smile. "Kathleen, can go back to work anytime she desires. It seems now that we are settled into our new church home, she has taken on a lot of responsibilities as the pastor's wife."

I bit the inside of my cheek while holding up the pitcher of sweet tea. "Anyone need a refill?"

Everyone shook their heads so I sat down. I unfolded the napkin, placing it on my lap.

Gran chewed thoughtfully and then looked over at me. "Kathleen, how is Lori doing? We don't hear much from her, other than what Kim tells us, which isn't much."

Matthew barked out a laugh. "Seems like that boss of hers has her working twenty-four seven. We hardly see her anymore."

Gran shot Matthew a look before looking at me.

"Matthew is right. We haven't seen her in months."

Gran frowned. "She doesn't go to your church?"

I shook my head. "She came the first Sunday Matthew preached but hasn't been back since then."

Gran frowned before picking up her fork.

The rest of the conversation over dinner was centered around Matthew's job and how many new members had been added since he arrived.

That night after we all went to bed, I couldn't sleep. My mind raced with thoughts of what Gran and Bumps would think of tomorrow's Sunday service.

Sleep finally found me. I dreamed strange dreams that night which left me on edge the next morning.

CHAPTER 37

$\mathcal{J}$ cut my eyes at Gran as the praise team finished their number in a cloud of smoke. The fog machine was doing double duty today and I caught Bumps coughing quite a bit.

The lights were raised as Matthew took the stage to deliver his sermon.

Matthew's sermon had been on giving. It was a topic he taught quite a lot lately. I was hoping he would preach on something else, especially since Gran and Bumps were in the audience, but I was sorely disappointed.

I could not put my finger on it, but lately Matthew's sermons left me more and more uneasy. I didn't want people coming to church to think all we wanted was for them to give money. I wanted people to come to church to experience what God could do in their lives.

Gran and Bumps had brought their nice clothes for church. The dark green dress which Gran wore and the black suit and red tie that Bumps had on were usually reserved for funerals.

After Matthew said the prayer, he headed up the aisle to greet the members as they left.

The lights came back up and I gathered my purse and helped Gran stand up as everyone made their way to the door.

"People sure are in a rush." Bumps stated.

I nodded. "They are trying to get out before the lunch rush gets to the restaurants."

Gran frowned and glanced at her watch. "Lunch rush? It's only eleven thirty."

I nodded. "And traffic is horrible any time of the day. Which is why I made Marry Me Chicken in the crockpot before we left. Once we get home all I have to do is heat up some rolls and we'll eat."

Gran grabbed Bumps arm for support as we walked up the aisle. Nancy Bridges, one of the women in the church, gave me a wave and made her way over to us.

"Kathleen, these must be your grandparents that you were telling me about." She stuck out her hand. "I'm Nancy Bridges. I help with the women's Bible studies and anything Kathleen needs help with."

I laughed. "Nancy, this is my grandfather, William Johnson and his wife, Betsy."

When they shook her hands my grandfather laughed. "Call me Bumps, it's what Kathleen has called me since she was a little girl."

"And I'm Gran." Gran gave Nancy a sincere smile.

Nancy beamed as she looked between us. "I know you are so happy to have them visiting. It's hard to get together with family when they live out of state."

Gran nodded. "We've really missed Kathleen. Seems like ages since we saw her."

Nancy nodded. "And Matthew."

Gran frowned.

"You must miss Matthew too." Nancy chortled.

I nodded quickly. "They do. Thanks for coming over and saying hi. We're going to try to hit the road before the traffic gets crazy."

Nancy gave me a look that said it was too late for that. She smiled and said her goodbyes.

We finally made it to the door and Matthew gave them both big grins. "So Gran and Bumps. What did you think?"

Bumps smiled and nodded his head. "Quite a production. We're not used to seeing something like that."

Gran pressed her lips into a thin line and muttered, "Production indeed."

Matthew didn't hear Gran but preened a little under Bumps' words of praise.

"We're headed home. How much longer do you have to be here?" I asked.

Matthew sighed. "Go ahead and eat without me. The elders wanted to have a quick meeting. Something to do with a new project. They said it wouldn't take me long." He gave me a quick kiss on the cheek.

The drive home was relatively quiet except for Gran and Bumps remarking about the driver's on the interstate.

By the time we got home, the chicken was done and I quickly popped some rolls in the oven to heat up.

We sat down at the table and Bumps said grace.

Bumps took a bite and smiled. "This is good, Kathleen."

I smiled. "Thanks, Bumps. It's a quick recipe that I can throw together if needed."

Gran nodded. "Bumps is right. It's good. Everything you've made is good."

That did my heart good, hearing Gran say something nice.

She cleared her throat. "So Kathleen, have you thought any more about nursing?"

I shrugged. "To be honest, I'm not sure. To get the hours that Matthew wants me to work is nearly impossible. A lot of nursing jobs are twelve hour shifts and even if I do an eight hour shift, that won't fit around the commitments I have at church."

Gran nodded slowly. "It looks like you are both doing well out here. Beautiful house, huge church, and Matthew seems to be making a lot of money."

I nodded. "They just gave him another raise. He keeps bringing in new members and the church is pleased."

"What kinds of ministries does the church offer?" Bumps forked some chicken in his mouth.

"A lot. There are children's ministries, and Bible studies for me and the other women. The high school students and college age students do volunteer work."

Gran perked up. "Oh, really? Do they go to homeless shelters or the food banks?"

I shook my head. "Not exactly. Right now they are helping at the animal shelters. But I did bring up at the last committee meeting that we should be doing more missionary work. Like you said, volunteering at the food bank and serving food at the homeless shelter. I even suggested the older students volunteer to tutor less advantaged students in the city."

Gran smiled. "Those are wonderful ideas. What was the feedback?"

I took a drink of my tea. "They will think about it." I had a feeling it was code for no way. I'd brought up tons of ideas and every one had been turned down. They claimed they didn't want to put the kids in a dangerous situation.

When I brought it up to Matthew he agreed with the committee.

"So how are things back home?" I desperately wanted to change the conversation.

"Everything is going well. I hope to have a very productive garden his year. Too bad you won't be there to help me can." Gran stated.

My stomach dropped a little. I looked over at Bumps. "Everything working right on the farm? I know the last time I visited, you were having issues with the tractor."

Bumps wiped his mouth with his napkin and nodded. "That sucker is running fine after Deacon fixed it for me. Don't know what I'd do without that boy."

I froze. Surely I had heard wrong.

I cleared my throat. "Deacon? Deacon Wilson?"

Bumps smiled, nodded, and kept eating.

I cut my eyes at Gran.

She gave me a warning look so I knew better than to say anything bad about Deacon in front of Bumps.

"So Deacon's pretty handy with tractors?" I kept my tone neutral.

Bumps nodded. "Sure is. He even baled hay. There is nothing that boy can't do."

I snorted. "Except finish college."

Gran snapped her head in my direction. "Kathleen Johnson. What a thing to say. Just because someone didn't finish college doesn't make them any less than anyone who did finish."

Bumps stopped eating and looked at me.

My face heated with shame. I swallowed hard. "I'm sorry, Gran. I didn't mean it…"

She cocked her head at me. "Then how did you mean it?"

I opened my mouth but nothing came out. Even if I didn't like Deacon, I had no business talking about him like that. I certainly hadn't set a good example as a pastor's wife.

I nodded. "I'm sorry. Deacon and I haven't always had a . .. an easy relationship. He tends to not be as nice to me as he is to you both."

Bumps nodded. "I think Deacon has had a hard life. Sometimes things in our past mess us up, makes us think we aren't good enough or deserving enough of a good future. The fact is Deacon never had a father around. All boys need a good father in their life. It helps them become good men."

I nodded. "I'm sorry, Bumps. You're right. And I'm blessed to have you and Gran as my parents. Without you two I don't know where I would be." My voice cracked with emotion and Gran took my hand.

Matthew burst into the room. "Sure smells good in here. Please tell me you saved some for me."

Bumps laughed. "It's really good, Matthew. Better get some while you can."

I stood and fixed Matthew a plate while he chatted up my grandparents.

When I sat down I realized the atmosphere had shifted. Once again my anxiety was back.

I glanced over at Gran and her expression had become strained. It was then I realized that Gran seemed to shut down whenever Matthew came into the room.

It was then I realized that to Gran, Matthew was the intruder.

CHAPTER 38

*M*y grandparents flew back two days earlier than planned. Aunt Kim and Uncle John had to go back early due to an unexpected issue at work, so my grandparents decided to leave with them.

I hugged Bumps tight before he walked into the airport. When I hugged Gran, she seemed like she didn't want to let me go.

I barely made it home because my heart was heavy. Thankfully Matthew was already at the church, which meant I had the house to myself.

That day I sat in the sitting area in my bedroom and poured over my Bible and prayed.

We had everything, but still it felt empty.

I pulled out a notebook and wrote down some ideas that I wanted to discuss with Matthew. I really wanted the students to start getting involved in the community. One great way would be to help out the older members in our congregation who no longer could travel to church. While the service was broadcast on TV, they still needed to be in the company of others.

I grabbed my phone and called Matthew's secretary, Donna. She picked up on the first ring.

"Hey, Donna. It's Kathleen."

I could see the smile on her face. Donna was always smiling, no matter what the conversation was about.

"Hello, Kathleen. How are you?"

I nodded. "I'm great."

Her tone was annoyingly nice. "I'm so glad to hear that. Matthew said your grandparents are visiting. What a wonderful treat."

I rolled my eyes against the sugary sweet tone in her voice. "Yes, they left today. Look, I was wondering if you could email me the addresses of our older congregation who no longer attend due to health issues."

She chuckled. "Why in the world would you want that?"

I bristled at her words. "I would like to see about visiting them. To see if they have any needs the church could help with. Like grocery shopping or maybe even picking them up and bringing them into church."

She gasped. "That's a great idea. The more members we have in the service, the more likely they'll give toward the building projects."

I narrowed my eyes. "Or maybe they could just be encouraged by the Word of God."

She laughed. "Of course. I'll check our records and send the addresses by the end of the day."

I nodded. "Perfect. Thanks so much, Donna."

I could picture her in her chair nodding with a plastic smile on her face. "Of course. Talk to you later."

As soon as the call ended, I got on my computer and began to make a list of needs for our older members.

Donna sent me the email quicker than I anticipated. Before noon I had the list of our older members which I quickly printed out.

Sitting down at the kitchen island I grabbed my phone and called the first name on the list.

An older man answered.

"Hello, Mr. Beck. This is Kathleen Hollings from Elate church...."

A small growl erupted from the other end before Mr. Beck spoke. "Elate! I already told you that I'm not giving that church one more dime out of my pocket!"

I was shocked into silence. I finally found my voice. "Mr. Beck, I assure you I'm not calling about money."

He snorted. "When does that church not call about wanting more money?"

I cleared my throat and glanced down at his address. "Look Mr. Beck. I think there is some kind of misunderstanding. I was calling to see what we could do for you, as a church. I noticed that you've not been in attendance in quite a while."

He mumbled something under his breath. "I can't leave my poor wife alone. She's bedbound."

I nodded my head, understanding his situation. "Mr. Beck. I see from your address that you don't live very far from me. May I please stop by today so we can talk?"

I waited for his reaction.

"Fine." He gruffed. "But if you try to beg my wife for any more money, I swear..."

I shook my head. "Mr. Beck. I will make you a promise that money won't even come up in conversation."

What had happened between Mr. Beck and the church that made him so agitated?

"We'll see." He stated before hanging up on me.

I sat there, quite taken aback by Mr. Beck. If I was going to visit with him, I needed to bring a goodwill offering.

Heading into the kitchen, I made up two plates of chicken

casserole, pasta salad, and steamed vegetables that I'd cooked for dinner last night. I threw in some homemade sugar cookies and headed out to my car.

CHAPTER 39

*M*r. Beck had seemed suspicious enough when he opened the door to me. It wasn't until after I showed him my gifts of food that he opened the door all the way.

I watched him from my seat at the small kitchen table as he put away the food.

"I'm shocked that anyone from that church even showed up, let alone brought food." He narrowed his eyes at me before closing the refrigerator.

Clasping my hands in my lap, I nodded at him. "Mr. Beck, you'll have to forgive me. I didn't realize that no one has been checking in with you and your wife."

He barked out a laugh and then sat down at the table. "All that church wants is money. They knew my wife had heart failure two years ago and we stopped coming. Not one person from that church has stopped by or even called to check on her. The only time they call is to remind me I haven't paid my tithe and that I need to get caught up."

My mouth dropped open. "You're kidding?"

He glared. "Do I look like I'm kidding? My wife served on

so many committees at that church for years. After she got sick, they stopped reaching out to see what they could do for her. It seems like all these young members want to do is go to church to dance and have an experience rather than hear the Word of God."

"You know...."

But he interrupted me.

"I heard they have this new young pastor. All our friends have since left because of him."

All the blood in my veins froze. I couldn't believe what I was hearing.

"Why did they leave because of Pastor Hollings?"

He snorted. "Lots of reasons. He's money hungry. He talks of how everyone in church should sow a seed and give money so God will bless them. He never once talks of Jesus and forgiveness of sins." He shook his head. "I'm glad I left that church."

I blinked as shock rolled over me.

For months now, after every service I felt like something was off. While I told myself that Matthew's preaching was different than what I grew up with, deep down I knew something was wrong.

I blinked back the sting of tears.

"Mr. Beck, I'm sorry that this happened to you and your wife." I cleared my throat feeling just as guilty as Matthew. I was his wife, I should have confronted him instead of shoving away my concerns. Now look where it had gotten us.

"You look familiar. How long have you been at Elate?"

I swallowed hard. "Almost a year."

He nodded. "So you came around the time that new pastor arrived." He snorted. "I bet he has you fooled too. Look, I appreciate the food you brought by, but if you are here to get money out of us for Elate..."

I held up my hands and shook my head. "No, absolutely not. Money is the furthest thing from my mind. And I'm sorry that the church has treated you this way. I had no idea."

He nodded slowly and then looked at me. "Look, Miss. I appreciate you coming to visit. But can I offer you a word of advice?"

I nodded and smiled. "Of course."

"You seem like a genuine, sincere person who loves the Lord. And if I were you, I would run as far away from that church as possible. Before it destroys you as well."

That day as I drove back home, my heart was heavy.

I wanted to call Gran and confide everything I had learned that day, but I didn't.

The guilt I felt was enormous.

Matthew had started off so good. And now look where he was.

If only we had stayed in Augusta. A smaller church with a congregation that looked after each other and was not so focused on money.

We'd made a mistake coming here.

I'd made a mistake coming here.

CHAPTER 40

I stood stunned as Matthew glared at me after hearing about my meeting with Mr. Beck.

"Matthew, Mr. Beck is right. The church should not be hounding people for money. The church should be caring for its members."

He shook his head slowly. "I cannot believe you went to his house without telling me you were going. What did you hope to accomplish?"

Anger flared in my veins. "I had hoped to see how he was doing. Just because someone is old, you don't discard them."

He snorted. "Well, maybe if he paid his tithes on time, then the church would be checking on him."

My mouth dropped. I realized then that I was married to someone I didn't truly know.

"Stop looking at me like that. You always were so self-righteous. Thinking so highly of yourself and how I wasn't good enough. Well, look at me now. I'm on TV every week with everyone tuning in to hear me, and what I have to say." He shook his head. "You know, Kathleen, I think you are jealous of my success and are trying to tear me down. It's not very Christian you know."

My eyes grew wide. "Christian? What's not Christian is telling everyone to give you money to build some building. What's not Christian is having a concert every Sunday morning to entertain the crowd instead of worshiping God. What's not Christian is not loving your neighbor, even when they get old."

He walked over and stuck his finger in my face. "Don't you dare preach to me. Don't forget who I am."

Sadness washed over me. I shook my head. "I know who you are Matthew. You're lost."

He looked at me and snorted. He grabbed his jacket and threw it on.

I frowned. "Where are you going?"

He grabbed his keys. "I'm going over to a friend's house. While I'm out, you should do some self-reflecting. I am the one who put us in this situation. You have a beautiful house, a respected position as my wife, and a life that most envy. Think about that before you lose it all."

He slammed the door behind him.

Devastated, I crumpled to the floor. Tears streamed down my face. I buried my face in my hands and prayed to God to give me the wisdom of what to do. And the strength to follow through.

CHAPTER 41

*M*atthew didn't come home that night until late. I wasn't asleep but kept my eyes closed. I couldn't bring myself to talk to him.

When I finally drifted off to sleep, I had nightmares about trying to get to my grandparents' house, but couldn't find it.

The next morning I woke up to an empty bed. Matthew had gotten up early and left, probably to go to the church.

I headed into the kitchen and made myself a cup of coffee. I'd prayed a lot in the last twelve hours. I didn't know what to do and I needed some direction.

My cell phone rang and I quickly answered it hoping it was Matthew. We needed to talk.

"Hello?"

"Mrs. Hollings?" A familiar voice was on the other end.

"Yes, this is Kathleen."

The woman sighed. "Kathleen, this is Mrs. Green from…."

I smiled. "From Augusta. Hello, Mrs. Green, it's wonderful to hear from you again."

A brief stretch of silence had my instincts on edge. "Is everything okay?"

Mrs. Green sighed heavily. "Kathleen, I don't know how to say this…"

My stomach dropped. "Say what? Is something wrong?"

I couldn't handle any more bad news.

"Kathleen, I have always liked you. I think you are a genuine person."

I shook my head. "You're the second person in a week that's called me sincere, right before hitting me with some bad news. I'm not sure how much I can take."

Mrs. Green cleared her throat. "May I ask a personal question?"

I nodded "Sure." I felt like the ground under my feet was shifting.

"Kathleen, I was in the church office cleaning out the old filing cabinets to make room for our new pastor."

I frowned. "Has it taken this long to get a pastor? I thought Matthew had someone lined up."

Mrs. Green snorted. "Matthew wasn't very forthcoming. The person he nominated wasn't even interested in the job. He had already taken a job in South Carolina."

I nodded my head slowly realizing Matthew had not been forthcoming. "I had no idea. I'm sorry. I know leaving so quickly left you in a bind."

Mrs. Green barked out a laugh. "It may seem that way, but I think it was a blessing in disguise."

I frowned "What do you mean?" I tried to brace myself for what she was about to say.

"Kathleen, I think you need to talk to your husband about his so-called seminary degree."

I didn't think I could feel any more betrayed but I was wrong.

"Mrs. Green, what are you talking about? Matthew completed his seminary online once we got to California."

There were a couple of beats of silence.

"Did you see the diploma?" Mrs. Green asked.

I shifted in my seat. "Not exactly. Matthew said it came in the mail and that he kept it on file at the church."

Mrs. Green muttered something I couldn't understand.

I felt like I was living in an alternate reality.

"Kathleen, the reason you never saw a diploma is because there isn't one. Matthew never completed seminary school."

I shook my head. "No, that's not true. Why would you say something like that?"

Mrs. Green cleared her throat. "Because when I was cleaning out the files in the church office, I came across a letter from the seminary school he said he was attending. Matthew got kicked out of school. He lied to us about still going to seminary school. I have a feeling the reason he got another job so quickly was to keep us from finding out."

The enormity of what she was saying crushed me. I honestly thought I would crash through the chair and onto the floor.

"Kathleen? Mrs. Hollings?"

I finally found my voice. "I have to go. Thank you for calling."

I ended the call before the tears could fall.

CHAPTER 42

"*How* ow could you not tell me? How could you lie about something like this?" I stared up at the man I had married and never really knew.

Matthew had been shocked that I had found out about his secret, but after a few minutes he recovered quickly.

He cast a glance at me and shook his head. "Kathleen, I didn't tell you because you wouldn't have come to California with me. You would have insisted we stay in that godforsaken small town, and I couldn't take it anymore. I was meant to be more. A lot more. And look at me now."

I shook my head. "Being a pastor is not to put yourself on a pedestal. It's to become less of yourself and become more Christlike. It's to preach the gospel to a lost and dying world. Not preach about giving money to make yourself rich."

In that instance his eyes changed, he looked quite different than my husband. "Don't you dare preach to me. You have enjoyed the fruits of my work just as much as I have."

I gaped. "I don't even know who you are anymore."

He snorted. "I'm the man you wanted me to be. I gave you everything, and here you are biting the hand that feeds you."

I gripped the kitchen island. "The church has to know the truth. They have to know you failed out of seminary."

A slow smirk settled on his lips. "Kathleen, you are so stupid. They already know. They offered me the job when my parents went to talk to them about hiring me."

I swallowed hard. "So your parents bought you a position at the church."

He shrugged. "I like to think about it as investing. This church is a progressive church which doesn't care about things like seminary schools, or validation. They care about someone who has the gift of speech and can bring the numbers in. That's how we change the world."

I studied the floor. "No. You change the world by telling people the Gospel. Not conforming to the world. Since you've been the pastor, I have not heard one sermon about salvation. All I've heard is you preach about sowing a seed and reaping money." I pointed my finger at him. "What you preach is heresy."

He grabbed my arm and shoved me back against the kitchen sink. "I would watch it if I were you. I am a very important person in this city, and I can make things disappear that irritate me. You wouldn't want to do that, would you Kathleen?"

Fear made my blood run cold.

I was trapped in my house with the devil himself.

How had I been so blind?

He released me and a smile swept across his face. "I'm going out to the country club. Don't wait up."

He strolled out the door leaving me standing in the rubble of a destroyed marriage.

I didn't remember going to my bedroom and collapsing on the bed in tears.

In anguished I cried out to God.

"I don't understand. I tried to live a life, following you. I tried to make you proud. How did I end up here? Dear God, why did you leave me alone?"

In the silence I cried myself to sleep.

When I awoke, it was dark outside. I sat up and headed into the bathroom. Glancing in the mirror, I didn't recognize my own reflection.

"God, please help me. Tell me what to do." I closed my eyes and prayed.

My cell phone began to ring, and I ran down the hallway into the kitchen.

I grabbed the phone. "Hello? Matthew?" I answered without even looking at the identity of the caller.

"It's Lori."

Relief flooded through my body. "Lori, thank God it's you. Are you home? I need to come over and talk to you."

"I'm home, but I have company. Right now is not a good time." Her voice was barely above a whisper.

I shook my head. "Something horrible has happened. I need to talk to someone I can trust." I glanced on the kitchen island, looking for my keys.

"No. that's not a good idea. I'm not available."

I froze. While I hadn't seen Lori in a while, whenever we talked on the phone she was her usual outgoing self who loved to talk about all the great things going on in her life.

She was acting really out of character.

"Lori, is everything ok?"

She chortled. "Of course. Why wouldn't it be?"

I frowned. "You're the one who called me. Is something wrong?"

She cleared her throat. "No. Not at all. I had some time to kill before my boyfriend came over and thought I would call.

But it seems like he showed up when you answered. Sorry to bother you. Have to go."

She ended the call.

The hair on the back of my neck stood up.

Something wasn't right.

While I had dismissed my instincts where Matthew was concerned, I had now learned my lesson. Grabbing my keys and my purse, I raced to my car.

CHAPTER 43

I pulled up to Lori's house and blinked several times. I couldn't believe what I was seeing.

Matthew's car was in the driveway.

He had come over to Lori's to try to get her to side with him.

I got out of my car and hurried up the driveway. With each step, questions tumbled around in my mind.

Why would he even try to talk to Lori? She'd not been over at the house in months.

Why would he think he could get her to side with him? She was my family, not his.

Why was this whole idea of confronting him here making my hands tremble?

Raising my hand to knock, the voices inside made me halt.

I pressed my ear to the door; I could hear laughing.

Surely Lori wouldn't be laughing with Matthew.

Stepping into the flowerbed, I peered through the living room window. My heart nearly stopped at what I saw.

Lori had her arms around Matthew's neck pulling him in

for a kiss. They were both laughing and kissing as he pulled her shirt over her head.

I screamed.

They turned and gaped at me in surprise.

"How could you?" I screamed at both of them.

Lori ducked behind the sofa and Matthew glared at me for interrupting their foreplay.

Hurt and anger rushed through me so hard that I thought I was having a heart attack.

Suddenly the door flew open with Matthew standing there with his shirt unbuttoned.

"Are you stalking me now? Showing up uninvited?" He glared.

I opened my mouth to try to talk but I couldn't form a word.

"If you know what's good for you, go home and make sure the house is clean before I get home. My parents are coming over tomorrow." He slammed the door in my face.

Clutching my stomach, I threw up in the flowerbed. I wiped my mouth, and got back in my car.

I didn't remember driving home, but somehow I managed. In a haze, I went to the computer and typed up a letter to the church and sent it out to all the members stating how Matthew did not finish seminary. I apologized and even signed my name to the email before I hit send. I felt it was the least I could do to warn them of the wolf in their own midst.

I pulled out a small bag and began packing a few things. I left the designer clothes and shoes that Matthew had given me in the closet. I packed my Bible and the picture of Gran and Bumps I had in my drawer.

It was already nine o'clock. I took inventory of the cash I had in my wallet, which was three hundred dollars. I pulled out the debit cards that went to our joint account and left them on the counter. It might take me a couple of days but if I left now I could make it to Georgia by Thursday.

I grabbed a bottle of water out of the fridge and stuffed it in my purse. Pulling off my wedding ring, I placed it on the counter beside the debit cards, and took one last look around the house many thought was perfect.

To me it only felt like one big illusion, just like my marriage to Matthew.

Grabbing my things, I tossed them in the backseat of my car and started the engine.

I didn't even look back before pulling out of the driveway.

It took a little over six hours to make it to Las Vegas. Before I was even out of Montecito, Lori was blowing up my cell phone. I didn't bother picking it up. What could she say that would make things better?

Lori was the closest thing to a sister that I had, and she had betrayed me in the worst possible way.

I stopped for gas in Las Vegas and was still too wired up to think about getting a hotel for the

NIGHT. So at three a.m. I continued driving. By the time I made it to Albuquerque the adrenaline

BEGAN to wear off and I pulled over into an empty parking lot to close my eyes.

I WAS JOLTED AWAY by a truck horn. I glanced around and realized I had slept for three hours.

My stomach rumbled but I felt too nauseated to eat.

Instead I drank some water and continued on my trek to my grandparents' house.

Shame and guilt plagued me the whole trip. I knew they would be disappointed in what had happened and would be disappointed in me.

As the day turned to night, I glanced up at the stars, wondering if God would still remember me during this time and have some kind of mercy on my crushed heart.

CHAPTER 44

I drove back home to Gran and Bump's farm. It took me two full days to make the journey.

I had no idea what I would face at the farm, but it was the only place I had to go.

I pulled into the driveway around six in the morning as I spotted a light on in the living room. My heart almost broke.

I killed the engine and stayed in the car. I pulled my coat closer to my body to keep me from freezing in the cold morning air. I'd not listened to the radio as I drove so I wasn't expecting it to be so cold when I arrived. Maybe it had always been this cold. Maybe living in California had made me forget what winters were like in the South.

The front porch door swung open and a tall, imposing figure filled the doorway.

I sat up in my seat and squinted. It was too big to be my Uncle John. Maybe it was one of the neighbors dropping in for an early morning coffee.

The figure suddenly disappeared inside. I groaned. I couldn't stay out here forever. I had to go inside and tell them what had happened.

Gran had been right all along. Bumps too. How was I going to apologize and make it up to them? Would they still love me?

I swallowed what was left of my pride and opened the car door.

Stepping out into the cold morning air, I breathed in deep, letting the wind burn my lungs and ruffling my unbrushed hair.

I curled my toes up in my heels and quickened my steps to the house.

As I climbed the steps of the porch, each creak had my heart tugging with memories of childhood.

I glanced over at the rose bushes around the porch. They looked dead against the winter landscape, appearing as if they'd not been trimmed back in a while.

Now that I was back, I would have to remedy that.

I reached for the front doorknob but stopped. I curled my fingers into my palm and gritted my teeth. I knocked twice and waited for what was to come next.

The door opened slowly.

Gran was standing there in a long pink housecoat and holding a tripod walking cane in her hand. She looked at me and blinked.

"Hello, Gran." My voice cracked with emotion. I wanted to ask when she started walking with a cane, but figured we'd have all the time in the world to figure things out.

"Kathleen?" Her soft blue eyes misted over with tears. "What are you doing here?"

I swallowed the pain in my throat and opened my mouth. Instead of words, I was racked with sobs as tears flowed down my face.

"Oh dear, come on in." Gran patted my hand and stepped out of the way to let me inside.

The house seemed smaller and older when I stepped inside.

"Come on back to the kitchen so we can have some coffee." Gran smiled weakly.

I wiped my eyes and entered the kitchen. The aroma of coffee filled the small space.

"Sit. I'll get you a cup."

I shook my head. "I'll get it." I pointed at her cane. "Why are you walking with a cane?"

She snorted. "My knee keeps getting worse. The doctor says I need a knee replacement, but there's too much to do around here."

I blinked. "Worse? I didn't know you were having issues with it."

Suddenly the dark figure appeared in the doorway. My heart dropped when I realized who it was.

"Maybe if you answered your phone, you would have known about her falling in the airport." Deacon Wilson shot me a glare before refilling his cup.

My heart sank. I whipped my head around at her. "Gran, you fell?"

She brushed me off. "It's not a big deal."

Deacon leaned against the kitchen counter. "Someone bumped into her trying to catch their flight and knocked her down in the Atlanta airport. They had to get her a wheelchair to get her to your uncle's car."

I blinked. "Nobody called me."

Gran waved Deacon off. "They told Lori so she would call you."

I felt the blood drain from my face. "So she knew? She never called." If I hated Lori for sleeping with my husband, what I felt now ran deeper than just hate.

I would never speak to that woman again in my life.

Gran frowned and reached for my arm. "Kathleen, what's going on? I know something is wrong."

I nodded slowly but couldn't say anything. Every time I opened my mouth to speak, I couldn't force the truth out.

"You look worn out. Why don't you go to your room and rest. We'll talk when you get up."

Gran looked over my shoulder at Deacon. "Can you get Kathleen's luggage out of the car, Deacon?"

He said nothing but headed out the front door.

I stood and headed upstairs to my room.

The minute I opened the door, my driving across the country had caught up with me and suddenly I couldn't hold my eyes open.

Walking over to the bed, I laid down and closed my eyes, not caring if I ever woke up again.

CHAPTER 45

"You need to get up."

I pried my eyes open only to find it was dark in my room. I glanced at the window and realized I'd slept all day.

I sat up in the bed in my wrinkled clothes.

Standing at the foot of my bed was Deacon. Despite the dark, I knew it was him.

I could always tell when he was in the room.

"What are you doing in here?" I stood and shivered at the coldness in the room.

He snorted. "I came up here to check on you. Your grandmother is worried about you since you slept all day. She was supposed to go to her doctor's appointment but canceled because she wanted to be here when you woke up." His heavy bootsteps headed toward my bedroom door.

"Deacon."

He stilled but didn't turn around.

"How are my grandparents?"

He propped his hands on his hips and looked at the ceiling. "You would know if you called them. You need to talk to them. And don't worry them. They have enough on their plates."

I walked over and grabbed his arm. "What do you mean? What's going on with them?"

He slowly lowered his head, looking at my hand on his arm. "Talk to them." He shrugged my hand off and walked out the door.

Flipping on the light, I looked around the room I had grown up in as a child. The same quilt was on the bed, messed up from where I'd slept. As I glanced around, I realized Gran had not changed anything in my room.

It was a room frozen in time.

A time when things were happy and my future was bright.

Sadness washed over me.

My bag was sitting at the foot of the bed. I opened it up and dug through it to find a sweater.

I remembered that I didn't pack a sweater when I was in California.

Standing up I went to my closet to see if I had left anything warm that I could wear.

There were some old T-shirts but nothing with sleeves. I grabbed the throw at the foot of the bed and threw it over my shoulders before walking downstairs.

The steps creaked more than I remembered. I suppose I wasn't the only one who had aged.

A dim light from the TV in the living room beckoned me.

I stepped inside and spotted Gran sitting in her rocking chair piecing together another quilt and listening to Perry Mason reruns.

She looked up when I stepped in the doorway. Her face lit up. "Kathleen. You're up. You must have been so tired. I was worried when you didn't get up for lunch."

I smiled and sat on the couch beside her. "I'm sorry to

JODI ALLEN BRICE

worry you. I was exhausted from driving all the way from California."

She frowned. "Why did you drive? Why didn't you just fly to come visit?"

I froze. "I...ugh..."

"Mrs. Johnson, I left Kathleen a plate in the stove before putting the leftovers away." Deacon appeared out of nowhere saving me from having to answer.

"Oh, yes. Kathleen, go in the kitchen and eat something. You must be starving."

On cue my stomach growled.

I smiled. "Yes. I'm starving." I wasn't sure I could eat but I wasn't ready to talk to Gran about what had happened.

I walked past Deacon into the kitchen.

I reached into the oven and touched the plate. "Ouch!" I pulled my hand back.

"It's hot." Deacon moved me out of the way and cut me with a look. He pulled the plate out with a pot holder and placed it on the kitchen counter. He moved out of the way so I could eat.

I grabbed a fork out of the kitchen drawer and took a bite of the meatloaf.

It was really good but I had no appetite. I swallowed and then set my fork down. I looked at Deacon. "Do you usually stay this late?"

He shrugged. "I stay as late as your grandmother wants me to." He cocked his head. "You didn't ask about Bumps."

I blinked. "I'm assuming he already went to bed." I cut my eyes at the time on the microwave. "It's only eight. He usually stays up until ten." I frowned.

"He gets tired early lately. That's why I'm over here more, in case you were wondering." He leaned against the wall and crossed his arms over his chest. "You look like you've been through something."

164

I looked away and nodded.

"Did he hit you?" His voice sounded gravely.

"Not exactly."

He cocked his head. "Are you planning on staying here?"

I swallowed the emotion in my throat. "I have no place else to go."

He nodded slowly. "A little advice?"

I wasn't in a position to shrug off any advice I could get. I stared at him.

"Tell your Gran as little as possible. She doesn't need to get upset about anything right now."

My heart nearly froze in my chest. "Is she sick? Is there something she's not telling me?"

He looked away. "I'll let her tell you. Just be careful how much you divulge about what's going on in California." He turned to leave and looked over his shoulder. "I always knew Matthew was a piece of crap. Never trusted a guy that's a little too perfect."

He made me smile at his accurate description of Matthew.

"Your Gran is sleeping in the guest room downstairs until her knee is better. I'll be back at eight. I was supposed to take her to the doctor, but now that you're here you can take her, and I'll help Bumps."

He left without saying goodbye.

I was glad. I didn't have the energy to muster up useless words.

Scraping my leftovers into the garbage, I then washed my plate.

I heard Gran's walking stick thumping along the floor. Turning around I smiled.

"I was about to come back into the living room after I finished cleaning my plate." Grabbing a clean dish towel I swiped it over the pretty yellow and blue chintz pattern.

"I see Deacon left." She eased into a chair.

"Yes." I put the plate away. "He said he would be back tomorrow." I looked over my shoulder at her. "He said he was going to take you to the doctor, but that I could since I'm here."

She smiled and stretched out her leg.

"Does it hurt?" I sat down at the kitchen table.

"Just sore. I think I don't need to see the doctor, but Bumps and Deacon said I do. It seems I'm outnumbered."

I nodded. "I agree with them. I'll take you so I can ask some questions." I swallowed hard. "I'm sorry that I didn't know about this. It makes me feel terrible." My life kept getting worse.

She patted my hand. "Oh, honey, don't feel bad. You didn't know. Besides, you are so busy with your life in California."

I looked away so Gran couldn't see the tears forming in my eyes.

"Why didn't you bring Matthew with you? Couldn't get away?" Gran asked.

I shook my head and got up from the table to get a glass of water. "Nope. You just get me."

Gran laughed. "I'll take it. How long will you be here? I need to get some groceries."

I shrugged and took a drink. "I don't know. A few weeks, I suppose." My heart beat fast in my chest. I had lied to Gran. I would eventually have to tell her I was staying a lot longer than she expected.

After helping Gran get settled onto the couch, I walked upstairs to bed where I laid awake until the early hours of the morning.

CHAPTER 46

I looked at my reflection in the mirror. My jeans sagged on my hips, I didn't realize I'd lost weight since moving to California. I had only packed a limited amount of clothes with me and they were all casual.

I managed to find a yellow blouse with quarter length sleeves but it wouldn't be enough to keep me warm.

Slipping my feet into my sandals, I headed downstairs.

Gran looked at me over the rim of her brown coffee mug. "Good morning, Kathleen. Hope you feel rested."

I nodded. "I do." I poured myself a cup of coffee and sat across the old kitchen table. "You still seeing Dr. Fenton?"

She nodded her head. "He said he has no plans on retiring. Since his wife passed, he's lonely and work keeps him busy."

I looked at the stove. "Want me to cook breakfast?"

She shook her head. "No dear. Lately me and Bumps just eat some cereal. He's already had his and is out in the barn with Deacon. You should say hi before we leave."

I stood and grabbed my cup. "I'll do that right now."

Heading out the back door, I made my way to the barn. I

braced myself against the cool morning air. Maybe I could talk Gran into stopping at the boutique in town so I could buy something warm.

I spotted Deacon working on the tractor while Bumps stood by watching his progress.

My grandfather spotted me and lit up. "Hey, Pumpkin!" he held his arms out for me and I hurried into them.

I clung to him and inhaled his familiar scent. He always smelled of coffee and hay in the mornings. Later in the day, once he had worked, he smelled of clean sweat.

When he pulled back he looked down at me. "What a surprise when I woke this morning. I waited around a bit to have coffee with you, but I had to get started on my day."

I nodded in understanding. "I understand, Bumps." I cut my eyes at Deacon. "I see you have help out here."

He nodded. "Deacon's trying to get this old tractor to run again."

I frowned. "Why? It's late in the season. Everything has been harvested or cut."

He barked out a laugh. "I'm going to hook it to the trailer and move some fencing stuff."

I laughed. "Fencing? What for?"

His face lit up. "We're going to start raising some sheep."

I frowned. "Sheep?"

He nodded. "Sure am. Deacon, here, is going to help me with them. It's a joint project."

I looked over at Deacon. "Really? I wasn't aware that Deacon was an expert in raising sheep."

Deacon didn't look at me but kept on working.

"Don't be late for Gran's appointment. She hates to be late." Bumps stated.

I laughed. "Oh, I haven't forgotten. I better get going. Need anything from town?"

"Peppermint candy." He winked.

"Got it." I cleared my throat and turned to Deacon. "Do you need anything?"

He stilled from working and looked at me over his outstretched arm. "Lemons for lemonade."

I snorted. "I doubt they'll have fresh lemons this time of year."

A look crossed his face, and it made me feel bad for laughing at his request.

"I'll see what I can do. Sometimes the grocery store gets some in from Mexico." I turned and headed back to the house where Gran was patiently waiting.

CHAPTER 47

"So she won't have to have knee replacement surgery?" I looked at Dr. Fenton.

"It's too early to tell. Right now I want her to rest," Dr. Fenton eyed Gran. "You hear what I said."

She sighed. "I've got too much to do. Besides, it's not like Kathleen is going to be here forever."

Dr. Fenton looked at me. "How long will you be here?"

I brightened. "I can be here for as long as Gran needs me."

He cocked his head. "I'd like her to take it easy at least three weeks. Four weeks will be better."

I nodded. "I can stay that long." Four weeks would buy me time before I had to tell Gran the truth.

"Good." Dr. Fenton smiled. He handed Gran a lollipop who brightened. "Too bad you're not staying Kathleen, I could use a nurse around here. Mrs. Williams is retiring in a couple of months and my other nurse, Mrs. Smith is going on maternity leave soon."

I started to open my mouth but caught myself. I shrugged. "Who knows what will happen in four weeks."

Gran stood with the assistance of her cane and slung her

purse over her shoulder. "We've got to head to the grocery store before we go home. Thanks, Dr. Fenton." She saluted him with her cherry lollipop.

We headed out the door. I waited patiently while Gran climbed in the car. I pulled out of the parking lot and turned on the street that would lead us to the grocery store.

I looked over at Gran. "If you give me a list, I can run in and get what you need."

Gran dug around in her purse and pulled out a grocery list written on the back of an envelope.

I parked and took the list from her.

"And here's my checkbook for the groceries." Gran signed a check.

I would have offered to pay but I was in no position to spend money.

"I won't be long." I opened the door.

Gran pulled out some knitting she always kept in her purse when she had to wait. "No rush." She smiled as her knitting needles went a mile a minute.

I hurried to the entrance and grabbed a shopping cart. I began picking up items, adding it to the cart, and checking it off my list. I forgot to get peppermint candy for Bumps so I turned down the candy aisle. After grabbing a bag I started for the check-out line but stopped.

Lemons.

I almost forgot the lemons.

I turned back to the produce aisle and found a small display of the citrus fruit.

Digging through the pile, I found enough good lemons and put them in a plastic bag.

As I watched the cashier scan my items, my mind drifted to Deacon.

Why had he wanted lemonade? The weather was cooler and called for hot chocolate. Not that he was a hot chocolate kind of guy. He was probably more like a hot toddy man.

I shook my head and paid for the groceries.

Deacon Wilson was the last person I needed to be trying to figure out.

First, I had to figure myself out.

CHAPTER 48

*A*fter running into the boutique to buy a denim jacket, we headed home. I settled Gran in the living room with some sewing to keep her occupied, I went into the kitchen to make everyone a quick lunch.

I found some leftover chicken in the refrigerator, and decided to make chicken-salad sandwiches. There were three sweet potatoes in the pantry that would make a great side as baked sweet potato fries.

After I made the chicken salad, I set the bowl in the refrigerator to chill while I made the lemonade.

I set about the routine of heating my water and sugar and cutting up the lemons.

Once I was done with everything I walked into the living room to let Gran know lunch was ready.

"I already made you a plate. I'm going to fix some sandwiches and take them out to the field to Bumps and Deacon." I wrapped up the last sandwich and scooped some fries into two containers.

"Thanks, dear. This looks great. I'm sure the guys will love it." Gran picked up a fry and took a bite.

I packed up the food along with a thermos of lemonade into an insulated bag I had found in the pantry.

"I'll be back soon." I headed out the back door.

The wind was blowing, and I burrowed down deep in my denim jacket. Fall was almost over and winter was coming soon. I would have to buy a proper jacket when I had time to shop.

I spotted Deacon pulling out fencing from the trailer while Bumps pointed at something in the distance.

When Bumps spotted me, he lifted his hand in a wave.

Deacon didn't stop working until I stepped in front of the trailer.

I put the insulated bag on the empty spot on the trailer. "I brought lunch. Hope you are hungry."

I pulled out the sandwiches and handed one to Bumps, and then one to Deacon.

Bumps thanked me but Deacon eyed me suspiciously before finally taking the sandwich.

Bumps took a bite and sighed. "This is really good, Kathleen."

I laughed. "Well, I have more. I made sweet potato fries." I placed a container in front of Bumps and one container in front of Deacon.

I frowned. "I forgot the ketchup."

Bumps shrugged. "Doesn't matter. Bet they are good without it."

I smiled. Bumps always had a way of making me feel better without even trying.

As I poured them both a plastic cup of lemonade, a weight seemed to lift from my shoulders and dissolve in the wind.

I stayed while they ate and listened to a story Bumps told about when he was a kid. Deacon snorted when Bumps told about the time his father whipped him when he caught him smoking behind the barn. I knew that Deacon could relate.

When they were done, I handed Bumps his package of peppermint candy.

He smiled. "Thanks, Pumpkin. And thanks for lunch."

I stuck my hands in my jacket pockets and nodded.

Deacon packed up the empty containers into the bag and handed it to me.

He leaned in and when he spoke it was under his breath. "You need to get a warmer jacket. It's supposed to be in the twenties next week."

I looked up at him under my lashes and nodded.

Waving goodbye I walked back home, with a lot on my mind.

CHAPTER 49

$\mathcal{T}$ ime passed differently in the country than in the city. I first noticed it when I went to college. In college there were tests, and classes, and events. In California, time moved even quicker. In fact, everything in California moved quicker. From the traffic to work.

Back at my grandparents' house in the country, time was noticeably different.

I didn't have blinds over my window to block out the light, just sheer white curtains. When the first rays of sun began peeking over the horizon, my body instinctively knew it was time to get up.

Though I was still tired emotionally, I knew I couldn't lie in bed all day long and nurse my wounds. I couldn't make Gran suspicious. I needed more time before I told her what had happened.

I showered and dressed before heading downstairs.

The smell of bacon was heavy in the house.

I frowned when I stepped into the kitchen. Gran was standing over the stove cooking breakfast.

"What are you doing? You're not supposed to be standing.

You need to rest that knee." I grabbed the spatula and herded her over to a chair.

"Ugh. I'm not bedbound, you know." She glared.

"But you are under doctor's orders." I poured her a cup of coffee and set it in front of her before flipping the bacon. I pulled out the carton of eggs. "Where is Bumps?"

Gran shook her head. "He went out to the barn. He'll be back for breakfast."

I pulled down three plates and then looked over at her. "Will Deacon join us for breakfast?"

Gran put her coffee cup down and nodded. "Yes."

I went about putting the cooked bacon on a paper towel and then frying up the eggs. I found the bread and put some slices in the toaster. If I got up earlier tomorrow, then I would make biscuits.

"Matthew must be missing you, Kathleen." Gran sipped her coffee.

I laughed. "He's got too much work to do to be missing me."

She placed her hand on the table. "Look, I know I haven't been supportive of your marriage with him and for that I'm sorry. There is really no need for you to stay so long."

I shook my head. "He knows I'm here and how long I'll be here so there is no need to worry about Matthew. If he needs anything, Lori can help him out." I spit out the last words.

"You know Kim told me that Lori never calls her anymore. I think something happened when we all came out to visit. Kim wouldn't tell me any more about it when I asked, so I stopped asking. I told her you have to let your kids live their lives." She gave me a sad smile.

I put everything on the table and then stuck my head out the back door. "Bumps, breakfast is ready." I called out.

Only a few minutes passed before both Bumps and Deacon were walking through the door.

Deacon had on jeans, a dark T-shirt, and had a ball cap pulled down over his head. Before he sat down at the table, he took his cap off and ruffled his dark hair which was in desperate need of a haircut.

"I'll say grace." Bumps reached for my hand and Gran's, which left me to hold Deacon's hand.

I held out my hand and he took it. This time his grip was gentle.

"Dear Lord, thank you for this food and how you provide for us every day. Thank you for bringing Kathleen back home for a visit. Help me and Deacon make progress on this fence. Heal Gran's knee and keep her healthy. Amen."

Everyone looked up and began eating.

In the silence of the meal around that small kitchen table, I felt, finally, at peace.

CHAPTER 50

The first few days I was at Gran's I settled into a routine. I cooked the meals and cleaned the house. When Gran tried to help, I refocused her on something that she could do while sitting down, like sewing or reading.

Deacon was over at the farm every day helping Bumps and by the end of the week, the fence was finally up. It was just in time since the sheep were going to be delivered on Monday.

Every day for that first week, Gran asked if I had talked to Matthew. I lied and said yes. The truth was my cell phone was dead and I had no reason to charge it. The only people I wanted to talk to right now were here in this house.

I didn't expect that Matthew would be calling. We had nothing left to say to each other.

Saturday morning as I was cooking pancakes, Bumps came in and smiled. "I haven't had pancakes in forever."

I shrugged. "I was trying to change it up. I added some blueberries to the mix."

His eyes lit up. "Even better."

I flipped the last pancake onto a plate and looked up. "Is Deacon coming?"

He shook his head. "No, he's at the church. We need to hurry up and eat and get on over there to help."

I frowned. "What's going on at the church?"

"We are painting the Fellowship Hall."

I cocked my head. "Inside or out?"

He grinned. "The inside. We want it to look good for the holidays. We figured since it's almost October, we need to do it now. The church has been putting it off for years." He sat down at the table and took a sip of his coffee. "Where's Gran?" He looked up at me.

"She didn't feel like pancakes so she had some toast. She's getting dressed for the day. I'm going to check on her. You need more coffee?" I held up the coffee pot.

"No, Pumpkin." He grabbed my hand and smiled. "It's good to have you home, Kathleen."

I gave him a smile and blinked back the tears in my eyes. I hurried out of the room before I lost my composure. I darted for the front door and ran out, straight into Deacon's chest.

He grabbed my arms and looked down at me. "You okay?"

I shook my head, unable to talk.

"Go to the barn."

I didn't argue but raced from the house in the direction of the barn. Once inside I leaned against the wood wall and closed my eyes.

Hot tears streamed down my cheeks and I wanted to scream.

Deacon appeared in the entrance of the barn and looked at me. Without saying a word, he pulled me into his chest.

I struggled in his arms, but he held me tight.

"Scream if you want to." He muttered against my ear.

All the emotion of the last few weeks where my life had fallen away, came rushing back like a roaring stream.

I buried my face in his chest and screamed.

I screamed until I didn't have any more energy left.

"I'll take Bumps and Gran to church."

I shook my head and I pulled back to look up at him. "They're expecting me to take them."

Deacon shrugged. "I can make an excuse. Besides, I'm already supposed to be helping."

I frowned and wiped my eyes. "Yeah, I thought you'd be there already. Why are you here?"

He looked over at the corner of the barn. "I need a ladder."

I followed his gaze and looked at the metal ladder. "Oh." I swallowed back my tears.

"Stay here until we leave. They don't need to see you so upset. It will only cause more questions." He walked over to the ladder, and picked it up with one hand.

He walked over to me and stopped. "Are you okay now?"

I nodded. "Thank you."

He stood there for a minute as if making sure I truly was okay.

When he walked out of the barn, I stared after him.

I waited until I saw Deacon drive away with Gran and Bumps. Whatever he'd said to them had appeased them because Bumps didn't come looking for me.

I only had a few more weeks left before I was going to have to come clean to them.

Maybe with the day to myself I could come up with a plan.

I walked back to the house and up to my room. I dug through the closet and found an old notebook with a lot of empty pages and took it downstairs with me.

Bumps had left the newspaper on the kitchen table and I opened it to the want ads.

Dr. Fenton's position for a nurse was not advertised yet which was good. I knew a position like that would fill fast.

I bit my lip and considered calling him up to apply right now before someone else got it.

I went upstairs and grabbed my cell phone. I plugged in my charger and went back downstairs.

Even if I didn't get the nursing position with Dr. Fenton, there were always positions at the hospital.

Getting a job wasn't something I was worried about. I was more concerned about how to tell my grandparents about my marriage being over.

I would have to have money for a divorce. I couldn't imagine Matthew contesting a divorce, not after everything that had happened, but I would need money to pay for an attorney.

By the time I finished making a list of what I needed to do, I glanced at the time. I headed upstairs to get my phone.

I unplugged it and noticed there were a ton of texts.

Bracing myself, I went through the messages from Lori. They were all the same, saying how sorry she was, how much she loved me, and the whole thing was a mistake.

I deleted them all without responding.

There was a missed call from our church in California. It was probably Matthew.

I took a deep breath and blew it out before hitting the button.

"This is Donna. The church has been made aware of the false rumor you have sent out to the whole church. I've been instructed to inform you that your membership has been canceled."

I gaped at the message. "Canceled? Is she crazy? Church membership isn't a magazine subscription." I spat out.

I went to the next missed message from an unknown number in California.

"Hello, Kathleen. This is Mr. Beck. I don't know if you remember me, but you visited with me and brought us some food. Please give me a call back as soon as possible."

My eyes grew wide. How had Mr. Beck gotten my number?

Curiosity got the better of me so I hit redial. He answered on the second ring.

"Mr. Beck. This is Kathleen. I just listened to your message." I waited patiently to see what this was all about.

"Yes, Kathleen. You certainly are a tough person to get to get in touch with. I just wanted to let you know, young lady, I don't like being lied to." His gruff tone had my heart sinking.

"I'm sorry that I didn't tell you who I was. After our conversation, I guess I was embarrassed to be part of a church like that." I admitted.

He let out a laugh. "Apparently you got over your embarrassment because I got that letter you emailed. Heck, all my friends did."

I gasped. "They did? I am so sorry that the church hired Matthew without knowing he had failed out of seminary school. I had no idea. You have to believe me." I cringed and covered my eyes with my hand.

"Oh, I do. And so do all my friends that used to attend. In fact, they are going to sue the church."

My eyes went wide. "What?"

He laughed again. "We're going to sue on the grounds that our tithe money was being taken on the false assumption that Elate was a true church. I don't know if we'll win, but that church isn't going to like the publicity it's about to get."

This wasn't going to be good.

"Mr. Beck, I didn't mean for that to happen. I just wanted the members of the church to know the truth." I was afraid that I had opened a can of worms.

"Don't worry, Kathleen. I'm sure their legal team will try

to squash this. But it will show the world what kind of church that really is. And it's not a true church. I'll let you go. Goodbye."

After he ended the call, I sat there stunned at what he'd just told me.

I looked through my missed calls to see if Matthew had called. Surprisingly he had not.

He was probably trying to lie low until everything died down.

Sitting back in my chair, I found it odd how quickly life could change on a dime. And how I could lose my footing if I wasn't careful.

CHAPTER 51

I shifted my weight in the pew as the pastor preached on the topic of how hardened people's hearts would be as we neared the end times.

After all I had seen, I wondered if we were on the cusp of it all.

Gran smiled and handed me a peppermint candy. I took it and tried to unwrap it as quickly as possible before popping it into my mouth.

The sweet taste sent childhood memories flooding back. As a child, Gran would always have candies in her purse to give me during the sermons.

As soon as the sermon ended, we all stood and then the pastor ended with a prayer.

"It's so good to see you, Kathleen." Mrs. Jones patted me on the hand. "I'm sure your grandmother is glad you are here to help her."

Gran nodded. "I sure am. I'll have to hurry and get better so she can get home."

My stomach tightened. I was running out of time to tell her the truth.

"Nice to see you, Mrs. Jones." I smiled and assisted Gran out the door while Bumps chatted with some of his friends.

I spotted Deacon at the back of the church. He quickly left before we reached him.

"Gran, how long has Deacon been coming to our church?"

She looked up at me in surprise. "Honey, he's been coming to church for a long time. I guess ever since he came back from college."

College. I still wondered why he left.

"How about we head home. That chicken won't fry itself." Gran patted my hand.

I grinned. "It's been a while since I fried chicken. But I'll do my best."

She frowned. "Matthew doesn't like fried chicken? What's wrong with him?"

I cringed when she mentioned his name. "Matthew doesn't like a lot of things." I muttered.

She studied me.

I smiled. "He says it's not healthy."

She shook her head. "What's that got to do with anything? I grew up on fried chicken and I'm still alive. If he wants to talk about something being unhealthy, he needs to talk about smoking. I see young people smoking up a storm these days and nobody's protesting that."

I stifled a grin at my grandmother as I helped her into the car.

I closed the door behind her and spotted Carl Manning, the local lawyer trying to open the tailgate on his truck while holding an armful of what appeared to be hymnals.

"I'll be right back, Gran." I mouthed to her and hurried over to help.

"Mr. Manning. Let me help you with that." I opened the tailgate and then grabbed a couple of the hymnals on top of the pile. "You're not stealing from the church are you?" I joked.

He laughed and shook his head. "No, Kathleen. These are the old hymnals that the church is donating to some missionaries overseas. They are always in dire straits for anything they can get, so we are sending these to them."

I smiled and flipped the page to "The Old Rugged Cross", Gran's favorite hymn. "That's a great idea."

He nodded and packed the hymnals in a large box to be mailed. "How is California?"

I froze and handed him the book. "Mr. Manning, can I ask a legal question and you keep it between us?"

He nodded. "Sure. What's the question?"

"What kinds of law do you practice? I know you've helped Gran and Bumps out with some legal issues surrounding their land a long time ago, but how big a scope do you practice?"

He shut the tailgate and looked at me. "I've done it all. Contract law, Family law, Divorce..."

I nodded and looked away. "I would really like to come by this week to talk to you if you have time in your schedule."

He nodded. "I'm pretty busy, but if you come first thing in the morning, I can talk to you then. Does that sound okay?"

I sighed. "That's perfect."

He grinned. "See you then. Hello, Deacon." He looked over my shoulder.

"Hi, Mr. Manning. I was just going to tell Kathleen that her grandmother is getting antsy."

The lawyer let out a laugh. "Well, don't keep her waiting. I'll see you tomorrow, Kathleen."

I stepped back and waited until Mr. Manning got into his truck and drove away before looking at Deacon. "I guess you heard that conversation."

He shoved his hands in his pockets and rocked back on

his feet. "I heard enough. You know, you need to talk to your grandparents."

I brushed the strand of hair away from my face and looked away. "I will. Just not yet. I don't want them to worry more than they have to."

I couldn't even comprehend the disappointment in their eyes when they found out the truth.

"I've been telling Gran her oil needs to be changed. That should be your excuse so she won't go with you. She hates going to get her oil changed. Says it takes too long and they're always trying to upsell you with a tire rotation."

I grinned. "Yeah, and the TV is always on one of those soap operas she hates so much."

He nodded.

"Okay, thanks for that." I turned to leave and then looked over my shoulder. "Are you coming for lunch? We are having fried chicken, with all the sides."

His face lit up, and I could tell it was something he hadn't had in a while.

"I was going to go to the truck stop and eat, but since you mentioned fried chicken, I just might drop by."

I nodded. "See you in an hour then." I made my way over to Gran.

When I slid in, Gran cut her eyes at me. "I saw you talking to Deacon. I hope you invited him for lunch."

I nodded. "I did."

Gran folded her hands in her lap. "Good. That boy isn't used to a proper meal. Not since his mother died."

I jerked my head in her direction. "Deacon's mother died?"

She nodded. "Yes, a while back. I thought you knew? That's why he left college. He came home to take care of her when she was diagnosed with cancer."

I was struck with a wave of sadness and regret. "I had no idea. I thought he left college because he got kicked out."

Gran pulled a face. "Kicked out? Deacon had really good grades."

I blinked and looked at her. "How do you know this?"

She pursed her lips together and lifted her chin. "Because I saw them when I went over to take a meal to him after the funeral. His mother kept his grades on the refrigerator."

I shook my head and started the engine. "I had no idea."

Gran snorted. "Well, you would know if you would ask. Can't just assume things, Kathleen. That's how mistakes are made."

I pulled out of the parking lot and onto the road. "You're telling me," I muttered

CHAPTER 52

$\mathcal{I}$ had convinced Gran to let me take the car in for an oil change. It was easy enough. Deacon had been right, she had no desire to go with me.

I finished my cup of coffee and looked across the table as Bumps and Deacon were finishing their breakfast of bacon and eggs. Gran looked out the kitchen door.

"I should be going. I won't be too long." I stood and put my cup in the sink. "I'll do the dishes when I get back."

Gran shook her head. "I can do the dishes. Oh and I want you to take Deacon with you."

I froze. "Why?"

Gran snorted. "Because they'll try to add something to the oil change. They try it with every woman who walks in. They won't try it with Deacon."

Bumps nodded. "Yes, Gran is right. I can spare Deacon. The sheep won't get here until this afternoon." He looked at Deacon. "You don't mind riding with Kathleen, do you?"

He wiped his mouth with the napkin and looked over at me. "I don't mind." He stood and took his plate to the sink.

"Gran, I can handle myself. Deacon doesn't need to go."

Gran shook her head. "You're taking Deacon. That's final."

I looked at Deacon and sighed heavily. "Fine. We'll be back soon."

The ride into town was relatively quiet until he spoke up.

"You need to talk to your grandparents." Deacon stared straight ahead.

I shifted in my seat. "I will. I just need to speak to an attorney first."

He arched a brow at me. "About a divorce? You know how your grandparents will feel about you getting a divorce."

I swallowed down my guilt. "I also know how they would feel about the whole truth about who Matthew is."

He narrowed his eyes on me. "Did he hurt you?"

I shook my head. "He never hit me if that's what you're asking."

He snorted. "Abuse comes in many forms. Physical is just one. It could be mental, emotional, financial…."

I held up my hand. "I get it. No need to lecture me." My eyes started to burn with angry tears so I blinked rapidly trying to hold them in. "I suppose you're going to tell Bumps where we really went."

He faced the road and slowly shook his head. "It's not mine to tell."

I frowned. For some reason, I trusted what he was saying.

I cleared my throat. "Deacon, I'm sorry about your mother. I didn't know she had died."

He said nothing but turned his face away.

"You could have come back to school after she died. I'm sure the school would have allowed it under the circumstances."

He let out a sad laugh. "The contract of the scholarship stated that if I left college for any reason, the scholarship would end."

I tightened my hands on the steering wheel. "That's not fair."

He turned to look at me. "Life's not fair. You should know that better than anyone."

I blinked. "Because my parents were killed in a car crash."

He looked away.

The rest of the ride was silent. When I pulled up at the attorney's office, we both got out.

"You're not going in with me." I stated.

He held out his hands. "I hadn't planned on it. Give me the keys so I can get the oil changed. Gran will look to see if they put a new oil sticker on the windshield. If it's not there, she'll ask questions."

I handed my keys to him. "Thanks."

He said nothing as he got into the car and drove off.

I turned and entered the attorney's office with a pit in my stomach.

CHAPTER 53

*M*r. Manning rubbed his chin after I explained everything.

"So, I need to at least get the paperwork ready for divorce. I'm sure he'll sign them. It's not like he wants to stay married to me, after everything that has happened."

"Kathleen, what do you want out of the divorce? As his wife you are entitled to something."

I shook my head. "Nothing. I want nothing. When I packed, I left the majority of my clothes in California. I didn't even take the expensive shoes he bought me." I touched my bare left hand. "I even left my wedding rings."

Mr. Manning snorted. "I'm surprised your Gran hasn't asked about your rings."

"She did. The other morning. I told her I took them off so I wouldn't lose them on the farm."

He studied me with sympathy in his eyes. "You need to tell your grandparents the truth. They'll understand."

I looked down at my hands clasped in my lap. "They'll be disappointed. I let everyone down. I should have listened to Gran. None of this would have happened if I had listened to

Gran. She knew what Matthew was and I didn't want to hear it."

Mr. Manning nodded. "Mistakes are part of life. It's what shapes and molds us into what we are. We grow from our mistakes."

I snorted. "I bet you've never had a client who's made a bigger mess out of her life than me."

He sat back in his chair. "Oh, I've seen people lose more than what you have."

I arched my brow in disbelief. "Really? Who?"

He stared at me. "Deacon."

His words settled over me. I cleared the emotion out of my throat. "Deacon had a mom."

Mr. Manning sighed heavily. "A mother who was never there for him because she was too caught up in her own grief of her husband leaving. He cocked his head. "Have you never talked to Deacon about this?"

His words took me back a little. "I'm not close with Deacon."

He frowned. "He's at your grandparents place all the time. And I saw you together at church. Didn't he drop you off here?"

I shifted in my seat. "It's not like we share secrets or anything. We might have gone to school together but we are as distant as any two people could be."

Mr. Manning nodded slowly. He grabbed the pen and the legal pad he'd taken notes on when we were talking and stood. "Let me see what I can get drawn up, and I'll let you know in a week."

I stood. The weight I'd been carrying around since I got here slid off my shoulders like snow off a roof. I stuck out my hand. "Thank you, Mr. Manning. I appreciate everything you've done."

He chuckled. "I haven't done anything yet. And just

remember, Matthew hasn't signed any papers. Don't let your guard down until that happens."

I walked into the waiting room and spotted Deacon standing there. "Oil change is done."

I smiled. "Thank you."

He held out the keys. "Are we going anywhere else?"

I shook my head. "No. Just going back home. Where I belong."

CHAPTER 54

*G*ran was getting stir-crazy from sitting in the house. So I had to come up with a solution.

I talked to one of her friends, Mrs. Galen, who was going to a quilt show a couple towns over. She had a wheelchair that Gran could borrow so she could push her around while viewing the quilts.

Gran was hesitant at first but once she talked to Mrs. Galen, she was excited to finally get out and about, even if she had to use a wheelchair.

"Kathleen, don't worry about a thing. I'll take good care of your grandmother." Mrs. Galen smiled at me.

"Yes, Kathleen, I'll be fine. Don't worry about me. It will take us over an hour to get there, and who knows how long we will stay there. I grabbed my checkbook in case I found a quilt I couldn't live without. Don't tell Bumps." Gran winked at me.

"I'm sure Bumps wouldn't care if you bought out the whole place. As long as you're happy." I stated. I waved as they pulled away from the house.

I wrapped my arms around myself and hurried back into

the house. Deacon was right. I needed to get another coat before winter fully arrived.

Bumps had already said goodbye to Gran before heading out to the pasture to check on the sheep that had arrived. He seemed to dote on them like a father dotes on a child.

I went into the kitchen and began tidying up the kitchen before heading upstairs. I checked my phone and noticed a missed call. It was from a number I didn't recognize so I didn't call back. Lately I had been getting a flood of calls from people trying to sell something.

I heard the rumble of a vehicle pulling up to the house. Frowning, I pulled back the curtain and spotted a white Toyota sedan.

Tossing my phone on the bed, I headed downstairs to see who it was.

I opened the door and froze.

"Matthew."

His eyes narrowed on me. "Aren't you going to invite me in?"

My stomach clenched as I opened the door to allow him access.

He stepped inside and ran his hand through his hair. Glancing around, he nodded. "Looks like everything has remained the same." He looked back at me.

"Not everything." I muttered and crossed my arms over my chest.

"I can't believe you left like that. Without talking things out." His expression shifted into one of devastation.

For a minute I was tempted to feel sorry for him. But then I remembered everything he had done.

"There is nothing to talk about. You've been unfaithful. Don't even try to tell me it was a slipup. The way you and Lori were carrying on makes me believe you two have been having an affair for a while."

He shook his head. "Lori was a mistake. It never should have happened."

I nodded. "You're right it never should have happened. But it just proves what kind of man you are. Someone who clearly has no business preaching. Not only are you an adulterer, you aren't even a real pastor. You're unqualified to even hold the office." I looked at him and shook my head. "I can't believe you lied to me for so long."

He lifted his chin and glared. "I bet it gave you great pleasure to send that email out to everyone in the church."

I sighed heavily. "No. It didn't. It was the hardest thing I have ever had to do. But it was the right thing. The church needs to know who is leading them." I turned and walked into the living room.

"Yeah, well, when you sent that email out, a lot of troublemakers who don't even attend anymore started making a stink. They are trying to sue the church and even got the news station to do a story on it. They are calling me 'the Wolf leading the flock of Elate Church'."

I turned and looked at him, "Really? Seems accurate." I didn't have it in me to fight anymore.

He grabbed my arm and turned me around ."You are going to come back with me and tell everyone you lied. You will come back and fix this mess you put me in."

I snatched my arm out of his grasp and stared at him in disbelief. "That I put you in? Are you delusional? You put yourself in that position. And for the record, I'm not going anywhere with you. I've already spoken to a lawyer who is preparing the paperwork as we speak." I turned to walk away but he grabbed me and spun me around.

He brought his arm back and swung hard, hitting me across the face.

Pain streaked through my head and I stumbled back cupping my cheek. I pulled my hand back and saw blood.

Fear, along with anger, filled my body until I was trembling with it. Before I could say anything, he hit me again.

"You stupid bitch. No one makes a fool out of me. I gave you everything and this is how you treat me?" He punched me in the stomach.

I crumpled to the floor, struggling to breathe. Pain shot through my body like lightening. His insults and curses filled my ears until it was white noise.

I crawled on the floor while holding my stomach. I had to get away from him.

For the first time in my life I thought I was about to die.

CHAPTER 55

*I*t was an animalistic growl that made my blood run cold. I covered my head to protect it from the next blow.

It didn't come. Instead Matthew howled in pain.

I pulled my hands away from my head in time to see Deacon grabbing Matthew by the back of the shirt. Deacon didn't hesitate but spun Matthew away and punched him in the face.

Matthew cried out in pain and stumbled backward. He wiped his face and pulled away blood from his mouth. "Look what you did to me! I'll sue you."

Deacon got in between me and Matthew. "Go ahead. You won't get anything."

Bumps came into the room and stopped. "What's going on here? Kathleen, what happened?"

I tried to speak but nothing came out, only sobs.

Bumps carefully got onto the floor beside me and cradled my face between his hands.

"Matthew hit her and kicked her in the stomach." Deacon growled.

Bumps jerked his head in Matthew's direction. "Is that true?"

Matthew lifted his chin. "You don't understand what she's done."

Bumps curled his hand into a shaky fist and glared. "I don't care what she's done. You don't ever hit a woman."

Bumps looked at me. "Let's get you up."

In a stupor I stood. It was like the world was in a haze and I couldn't make sense of everything that was going on.

"Bumps, wait. I have to say something." I gripped his hand for support, more emotional than anything.

"We can talk about this later…"

I shook my head. "No, now." I glared at the man I had thought I would spend the rest of my life with.

I stood and grimaced at the pain in my body. "Bumps, I haven't been honest with you or Gran."

Matthew smirked. "Well, look at that. Miss Perfect is a liar."

Deacon stepped forward with his fist raised ready to defend me.

"Wait, Deacon. I need to say this."

Deacon's arm slowly went down by his side but he never stopped glaring at Matthew.

"Bumps, I didn't come here for a visit. I came here because I left Matthew."

Bumps gave Matthew a seething look. "Has he hit you before, Kathleen?"

I shook my head slowly. "No. I didn't leave him for abuse. I left him because I found out he was having an affair. With Lori."

Bumps' eyes grew wide in disbelief. He looked over at Matthew. "Is this right?"

Matthew wiped his nose and sniffed. "It was a misstep. What's the big deal?"

Bumps looked at Matthew like he had three heads.

"That's not all. Matthew got kicked out of seminary school. He never graduated. He's mad that I sent out an email to the church letting all his members know about it."

Deacon barked out a laugh.

Matthew started to say something but from the look that Deacon was giving him, he thought better of it and shut his mouth.

Bumps shook his head. "Kathleen, why didn't you just tell us?"

I swallowed back the emotion in the back of my throat. "Because I didn't want to embarrass you or Gran. I didn't want to disappoint you."

He reached out and tenderly stroked my cheek with his calloused finger. "Pumpkin, we would never be disappointed in you. We love you and only want the best for you."

Matthew fisted his hands at his sides. "Kathleen, you have caused a lot of damage to my career. You need to come back with me to California and tell everyone you lied."

I shook my head. "No. I'm not going anywhere with you. I've talked to a lawyer and he's drawing up divorce papers."

Matthew sneered. "Divorce papers. I'm not signing any divorce papers."

Deacon walked over to the entryway and came back with a manila envelope. "Yes, you are." He opened the envelope and shoved it at him.

"What's this?" Matthew sneered.

"It's divorce papers." Deacon glanced over at me. "Mr. Manning tried calling this morning but you didn't answer. He waved me down when I passed his office and asked if I would take these to you."

I nodded.

"I'm not signing anything without having my attorney look at it. You'll try to take me for all I have."

I snorted. "I don't want any of what you have. I asked Mr. Manning to draw up papers saying I don't get anything of yours and you get nothing of mine. I didn't even bring my wedding ring with me when I left."

Matthew looked at me like he didn't believe me. He pulled out the papers and began reading each page. By the time he was done, he looked at me in disbelief. "What's your angle?"

I looked at him through the sting of tears. "I'm not like you, Matthew. I don't have an angle. I just want to be rid of you."

The look on his face was indescribable. I was certain that no one had ever said that to him.

"Fine." He slammed the papers down on the table. "Give me a pen."

Bumps pulled a pen out of his shirt pocket and held it out.

Gritting his teeth, Matthew took the pen and quickly signed his name to all the places marked for him to sign.

"There." He stood and lifted his chin. "To be honest, I'm glad to be rid of you too. Lori fulfilled my needs way better than you ever did."

Matthew didn't even see the punch coming. But when Deacon landed his fist to his jaw, Matthew screamed like a girl before picking himself up off the floor and scrambling out of the house.

No one said anything until Matthew's car was out of sight.

Deacon turned and looked at me. "Are you okay?"

I shook my head. "No, but I will be. I just need time."

CHAPTER 56

"*I*'m going for a walk." I said before bundling up in one of Gran's old winter coats. I still hadn't managed to find the time to buy one for myself. Not that it mattered. Since Matthew's visit I had kept away from church and town until my face could heal. The purple bruise that had been there was now fading to a light yellow.

"Kathleen, take Bumps with you." Gran gave me a worried look.

I chuckled. "Gran, I'm pretty safe. I don't need Bumps to go with me. Besides, since Matthew's visit, neither of you have let me be alone outside this house. I just need to get some fresh air."

Gran pursed her lips together. "I know. But I can't help but worry." She reached for my hand and gave it a squeeze. "I should have put my foot down when it came to Matthew. It's my fault I allowed you to marry that monster in the first place."

I sat down at the kitchen table with her. Taking her hand in both of mine I looked in her eyes. "Gran, none of this is your fault. I had some reservations, and I should have listened to my instincts. But I didn't. Instead of seeking wisdom from God, I got caught up in trying to defend the red flags I was seeing. So none of this is your fault."

Gran sighed heavily. "I talked to Kim this morning."

I stiffened.

"Kim knows about Matthew and Lori. She and John are shocked at the news."

My eyes widened. "How did they find out? Did you…."

Gran shook her head. "I didn't tell them. Lori did."

I couldn't believe my ears. "She did?"

Gran nodded. "She said she was sorry for having an affair with Matthew and that it was the biggest mistake she'd ever made."

I snorted. "I wish I could believe that."

Gran cocked her head. "You know, Lori has always been jealous of you."

I barked out a laugh. "Right."

Gran cleared her throat. "No, I'm serious. You've always done well in school and everyone loves you. You graduated with your nursing degree which was your dream. You are kind and compassionate and have always tried to live your life for God."

I sighed heavily and looked at the floor. "And look at how miserably I failed."

Gran lifted my chin. "Everyone fails, sweetheart. Life is full of lessons. One thing I want you to remember is to let go of your resentment toward Lori and Matthew."

I frowned.

She laughed. "I'm not saying forgive them now. You can be hurt for a while. But remember you have to forgive them eventually. I would hate for you to go through life letting this weigh you down."

I nodded.

"Oh, and Dr. Fenton wants you to work for him if you turn down that hospital position." Gran grinned.

I nodded. "Thanks for letting me know. Now can I go for a walk? I just want to go see the sheep."

She smiled and nodded.

I hurried outside into the bite of winter air. The holidays were coming up soon. Although I was usually excited for them, I knew this year would be different.

Gran's knee was healed and I had job offers which was great. The whole town knew about Matthew and what had happened, and they all rallied around me through sending me flowers, notes, and calling.

I had a feeling that Bumps had been instrumental in letting the cat out of the bag.

I'd spent my time healing from the physical and emotional trauma by reading my Bible and journaling my thoughts.

I snuggled down deeper in the coat and walked a little faster in the direction of the sheep.

I looked up at the overcast sky and wondered if we would get a rare holiday snow.

Topping the hill, I smiled when I saw the sheep all grazing on hay that Deacon had delivered yesterday.

I eased my pace so I wouldn't scare the sheep. I stopped and leaned against a tree. From the tree line, I spotted Deacon driving up on his all-terrain vehicle.

He said he bought it to help with the chores around the farm. But I knew better. He'd bought it to help Bumps get around the farm more easily.

I waved in his direction. He spotted me and drove over.

He killed the engine and got out. "What are you doing? Is Bumps with you?" He looked around.

I shook my head. "I needed to get out of the house and get

some fresh air. It took some convincing for Gran to let me go, but she finally complied."

He gave me a rare grin.

My face heated and I looked away. "So what are you doing out here?"

He shrugged. "Just checking to make sure the sheep have enough hay. It's going to get cold so I would like to herd them into the standing shelter on the other side of the hill to get them out of the wind."

I frowned. "Will they go on their own?"

He laughed. "Sheep like to be led."

I nodded. "I can relate."

We stood there in silence watching the sheep for a while before I spoke.

"Deacon, I wanted to thank you for what you did. If you'd not come in when you did, I don't know how far Matthew could have gone."

He looked at me for a second, and then nodded in the direction of the shelter. "Walk with me?"

I nodded and we walked side by side.

"I knew what Matthew was. In college there were some rumors that he wasn't the nice guy everyone thought he was. I should have warned you." He stuck his hands in his jacket.

"I don't think I would have listened to you even if you tried." I blinked and then stopped. "But you did try to warn Bumps, didn't you? That time I walked in on you and him in the barn. You two looked like you were having an argument. You were telling him about Matthew."

He nodded once. "Don't be upset with Bumps not believing me. Matthew was very convincing."

I narrowed my eyes. "Matthew is a wolf."

He chuckled. "Totally agree."

We walked on further.

"I need to apologize to you for how I treated you in high

school and college. I wasn't exactly nice to you when we were growing up."

I shrugged. "You were a little boy who had to grow up without a father. That's something I can completely understand."

He shook his head. "Doesn't make it right. I think I was jealous that you still had grandparents who took care of you. After my father left, my grandparents wanted nothing to do with me so it was just me and my mom. Life was hard for me, but it was harder for my mom. She worked really hard to provide and I always had a chip on my shoulder. I hope she knew how much I loved her when I took care of her during her last months."

I swallowed back the emotion. "I'm sure she did. Gran said your mom knew. Not many men would have done what you did."

Silence stretched between us.

"I saw you, in the courthouse, the day I got married." I looked over at him.

He nodded. "I wanted to intervene, but I saw Bumps and Gran, and I didn't want to embarrass them. I should have said something then. I'll regret not speaking up for the rest of my life."

I grabbed his arm and we stopped. "Please don't live in regret. Not for me."

He looked down at me with those dark eyes. Reaching out he brushed a strand of hair away from my face.

"Do you know what a treasure you are, Kathleen?" His deep voice seemed to sooth the edges of my pain. "When you left with Matthew, I would lie in my bed and pray every night to God that he would bring you back."

I swallowed. "You did? Why?"

His eyes softened and suddenly I saw him clearly.

"Because I loved you. I still do. I've loved you since we were in school together."

He dropped his hand and started walking.

I quickly caught up to him. "Wait, how did I not know this, Deacon?"

His expression was strained. "Because I didn't know how to show it. I barely knew how to show it to my mom. It wasn't until Bumps took an interest in me that I had an example to follow." He looked away.

"I'm sorry, Deacon. I wish I had been kinder to you. I wish I had known."

He gave me a slight grin. "You were kinder to me than I deserved."

I shook my head. "How?"

He shrugged. "The small things. Holding my hand at that Christmas dinner while Bumps prayed. Or making me lemonade when I was thirsty."

I wanted to shrink into the ground. "Deacon, that wasn't done in love."

He grinned. "Love is patient, love is kind. You were both to me when I didn't deserve it."

His words touched my heart. "I wish I had done more."

He cut his eyes at me. "Well, maybe once your divorce goes through you would go out with me."

I grinned. "What kind of date are we talking about?"

He pointed past the fence line that separated Bumps' land from the neighboring land. "You see that?"

I shoved my hands into my pockets. "Yes. That's Mr. Willis's land."

He shook his head. "Not anymore. I bought it."

I gaped. "Bumps must be paying you well."

He shook his head. "Not nearly enough to pay for that."

I looked at him. "How did you afford it? Bumps has

wanted to buy Mr. Willis's land for years but it was always too expensive. We couldn't afford it."

He cocked his head. "After my mom died, I was informed that she had a life insurance policy which named me as the beneficiary. So I made Mr. Willis a cash offer and he took it."

I smiled. "Really? I bet Bumps was a little mad that he didn't get it."

He looked at me strangely. "He wasn't. I think he thinks it will somehow end up in the family after all."

Suddenly the meaning of his words dawned on me.

"His land comes with a small cabin and I just bought some cows to add to my land. For all my life, I have always wanted some place to call my own. And a place to raise a family."

I looked at the land. "So do you think you can afford a family and a wife?"

He looked thoughtful and then nodded. "With the income from the truck stop I bought, I think so."

I jerked my head at him. "You own the truck stop? The big one on the interstate?"

He nodded. "Turns out mom's insurance policy was really big so I was able to buy the truck stop and this land as well. I've been living in the cabin and fixing it up before coming over here to help Bumps."

I crossed my arms over my chest. "So that's how you get here so early in the morning. And sometimes without your truck. You walk."

He grinned and his face lit up. "Want to see it?"

I nodded.

We walked in silence over the rolling hills of his newly acquired land until I saw the cabin come into view. I stopped and gasped. "Deacon, it's beautiful."

He shrugged. "It's no California mansion, but I like it."

I looked at him and smiled. "Who needs a mansion when

you have this little slice of heaven. You should plant a flower bed on either side of the steps. Gran has some pretty rose bushes that would look great right there." I pointed. "Oh and those must be apple trees. You will have loads of apples in the summer that will be perfect for canning. You also need to hang some ferns and petunias off the porch." I turned and looked at him. He stared at me with so much love it almost knocked me to my knees.

"Kathleen, I can't take you inside the house. Because once you step foot inside, I would never want to see you leave. My heart can take a lot, but my heart can't take that. So all I'm going to do is kiss you. And if you don't want me to kiss you, then stop me now."

I opened my mouth to give him ten reasons why it was a bad idea since I was still married.

But the words wouldn't come out.

His lips were soft and gentle on mine, and I found myself wanting to pull him closer. The kiss soaked into my heart and I wondered how I had never seen who he truly was. Thankfully, Deacon had more control than me and broke the kiss.

"I'm going to walk you home. And when your divorce is final, I'm taking you out on a date. Anywhere you want." His words were hoarse, and I could almost hear his heartbeat from where I stood.

I nodded.

"I can't give you the world, Kathleen, but I can give you my heart and I will never hurt you."

I smiled and reached for his hand. "That's enough. And more valuable than all the mansions in the world."

*K*athleen and Deacon were married three months after their first date. Neither Bumps or Gran were surprised by their relationship. Gran said she "knew all along" that Deacon was the one for her.

Deacon continued working his farm as well as helping Bumps with his.

Kathleen worked day shift at the hospital four days a week and made their cabin a home on the days she was off. By the time their first child came along, Kathleen cut her hours to part time. And when their second child arrived, she became a stay at home mom.

As the years passed, and her grandparents became unable to care for themselves, Kathleen and Deacon moved into the farmhouse to take care of them. For them it wasn't a burden, but a gift to care for the two people who had cared for them when they were young

Uncle John and Aunt Kim regularly visited. After five years of their marriage, Lori came to visit.

Kathleen hardly recognized her. She was broken from all the troubled relationships she had gotten into over the years.

She apologized profusely to Kathleen for causing her pain and said she had moved out of California to a small town in Tennessee where she had gotten involved in a local church. It's where she found forgiveness for all the mistakes she's made throughout the years. Lori finally settled down and married a single father of two little girls, whose wife had been killed by a drunk driver. Kathleen was happy for her cousin who was finally on the right path.

Matthew's parents, they had lost all their money in a Ponzi scheme. They were forced to move out of California to a town in Nebraska where Kitty had an aunt who took them in on her farm. The last anyone heard, they were both miserable but didn't have any other options.

As for Matthew, his church got into a lot of legal trouble for continuing to harass members for money. Despite this, he continued to preach two more years, until he ended up having sex with one of his congregants who happened to be underage. There were rumors he was in jail. Others said he was on the run.

Kathleen didn't care. All she knew she was living the life God always intended on her little farm with her family.

ABOUT THE AUTHOR

Jodi Allen Brice is a USA Today best-selling author of over thirty novels under different pens names. Jodi writes small town romance, cozy mystery and women's fiction with a touch of humor. You can find out more about her next release and appearances at http://jodiallenbrice.com

ALSO BY JODI ALLEN BRICE

Harland Creek Series
Promise Kept
Promise Made
Promise Forever
Christmas in Harland Creek
Promise of Grace
Promise of Hope
Promise of Love
Candy Cane Christmas

Laurel Cove Series
Lakehouse Promises
Lakehouse Secrets
Lakehouse Dreams

Stand alone novels.
So This Is Goodbye
Not Like the Other Girls

Harland Creek Cozy Mystery Quilters
Mystery of the Tea Cup Quilt
The Mystery of The Drunkards Path

Made in the USA
Columbia, SC
11 March 2023

13561008R00133